The Ventos Conspiracy, Volume 2: Confrontation

By
Jonathan Welsh

The Ventos Conspiracy 2

I dedicate this second book to my parents, my brother and his partner, my sister and her family, and again to my partner, Heather, whose invaluable help, unerring support and forbearance of my going on about "my book" (now plural!) was beyond the call of duty.

My proof readers (in no particular order): my friend and fellow conchologist Alison Effney, Heather and my friend Daniel Lewis-Dayle. Obviously, any mistakes which still remain are entirely down to me!

I'd also like to thank all my relatives, colleagues and friends from around the world who bought book 1.

Note: as some of you know, my original intention had been to publish this and volume 1 together as a single book. Ultimately though, I decided to split that novel into two halves. The action in this book continues straight on from the end of book 1 and, after this book, the adventures will continue in "The Ventos Conspiracy, volume 3: Paradox".

The Ventos Conspiracy 2

Chapter one – Return

The return flight to Ventos was uneventful, nothing showed up on the scans and the ship continued to function perfectly. The FPO remained dormant in the dirt box for much of the time – it clearly didn't like interstellar spaceflight and was much happier on a solid surface. As I approached the still icebound Ventos, it was obvious from the scanners that the mining operation was in full swing as the protective bubble around the area at the edge of the sea and the region around it was a hive of activity. All around the dome and on the central meteorite crater spike, there were fifty or sixty giant mining machines in operation. These were spewing out fumes and presumably extracting millions of tonnes of rock to be purified and made into the lethal mind controlling jewellery. The simplest solution to the whole thing would be to launch my one remaining nuclear missile at it and destroy it. However, that would be a great way to kill or maim hundreds of innocent people which I did not want to do. Therefore, in order to stop the mining, I needed to get into the dome.

As I got closer to the planet, I activated the camo drive and then programmed in a geosynchronous orbit so I could monitor the situation and look for a decent landing location. I stayed in orbit for an hour or so before I decided on an uncharacteristically flat ice field a few kilometres from the dome, just over the main summit of the mountains. These had now become majestic ice covered peaks with powerful winds and huge snow drifts and crevasses. Traversing these would be a job for an experienced mountaineer which unfortunately, I wasn't. I momentarily wondered if that was another training programme that I should have "borrowed" from The Union. Luckily, thanks to my thieving from them, the ship was equipped with all of the necessary cold weather gear I needed so at least in that regard, I would be prepared. Another plus was that the sun seemed to be shining a bit more powerfully so it would might partially recharge the ship's power cells which were somewhat depleted from the journey to the dead Earth and through the globule.

    I manoeuvred carefully towards my selected landing spot and landed safely despite the ferocious crosswinds - the advanced flight training courses had obviously paid off. I had deliberately parked in a fairly wide open space so that the heat signature from the engines would quickly dissipate in the freezing air. I stayed inside the ship for an hour or two, checking the temperature readings and the general disposition of the area. One of the last things I did before leaving was to grab a small bag which I filled with dirt for the FPO to stay in. As everything on my scans indicated that it seemed reasonably safe outside, I suited up into the internally heated white mountaineering gear, complete with inbuilt navigational system, grabbed my portable snow tent and activated the main airlock. At this point, the FPO eagerly jumped out of the dirt box, perhaps sensing it was home again. Due to its physiology, it would certainly find walking on the snow far easier than I would as its low profile shape and light weight meant it could do so without breaking the icy crust.

    The cold outside was intense, the wind was freezing and seemed to blow right through me and I started to shiver uncontrollably. It was utterly horrible for someone who hates being cold but it served a purpose in that any trace of my footprints would be erased quickly by the weather conditions. Despite my personal reluctance to go out, the FPO clearly thought otherwise as it leapt enthusiastically out of the ship and into the snow, squeaking as it did so. It skipped about clearly loving the cold snow and generally having a play, like a child enjoying their first snowfall.
    "At least you seem to like this shitty weather." I said to it wearily.
    Unsurprisingly, it did not reply.

    I closed up the ship and we set off across the ice field, the FPO following me diligently like a small pet dog. I had left the camo drive running so the only evidence of the ship was a ship shaped gap in the swirls of snow but these were so intense that you'd practically have to be on top of the craft to spot it.

The Ventos Conspiracy 2

I trudged along in the snow, accompanied by the manic FPO for what seemed like hours. I never liked the cold white stuff back on Earth especially as, with the climate change which had occurred, snowfalls in what had been the UK had become more frequent and powerful. Most of this was due to the North Atlantic conveyer having failed badly in the mid-twenty first century and once this happened, the climate of the UK had begun to change radically. Even the repairs the human race had made to the planet since had not quite reversed this and so there were still very bad snowfalls even in my time. In the end, I'd got so sick of it that I had considered moving to a warmer country but I'd never got around to it. Maybe subconsciously, my planned month in Australia had been a test to see how I would cope leaving the former UK?

Out here, almost alone and millions of kilometres from home, the snow just made it incredibly depressing and wet. It was also perishingly cold, the internal heat pads in the mountaineering gear could only just about keep my temperature above a safe limit of thirty six point four degrees Celsius so I was growing increasingly uncomfortable. Any malfunctions in that system could lead to another dose of hypothermia and that wasn't on my "to do" list - one brush with a cold death was enough for one lifetime. As I climbed higher up the increasingly steep slope, the temperatures dropped still further and the wind got even more powerful. Soon it was almost a

The Ventos Conspiracy 2

total white out situation but the built in navigational system in the snow suit kept me going in the right direction.

By now, even the FPO was beginning to tire, it's gambolling about was less frequent and intense. Every so often it would stop and watch me intently for a few seconds as if to say "Why exactly are we doing this?" – a sentiment I almost found myself agreeing with wholeheartedly. However, my stubbornness meant that I kept trudging onwards in the freezing conditions.

As the terrain grew more rugged, I kept going. Eventually, what seemed like hours later, it began to get dark so I decided to pitch camp. The portable snow tent was extremely useful and contained a very clever electrothermal heating system which fed back any body heat into the living space. As it was only meant for one person, I would be providing my own heating and the FPO could also help boost it too, just by being there. I selected what appeared to be a good spot to set up camp in a lee from the wind beside a particularly enormous boulder. It was probably ejecta from a previous meteor impact but it would do just fine as it was shaped like a boomerang. The concave side was the perfect size for the tent to fit in snugly. I stood about a metre away from the rock face and pressed the button. There was a small hiss and the tent spewed out from the backpack, filled out to the desired shape, attached to the rock and within thirty seconds, I had a habitable space. Before I climbed in, I set up the micro sensors on the outside of the tent to maximum intensity and connected them to my suit. If they were triggered and I was asleep, I would be awoken and able to make a run for it. Then I climbed in, followed by the FPO, which now somehow managed to look mutinous, and made myself comfortable. In less than five minutes, the inside of the tent was a pleasant temperature and so I broke out rations and feasted. The FPO snuggled into its little bag of dirt and went dormant. I decided against my sleeping pills, just in case I was discovered by The Union forces. I closed my eyes just as the last of the light drained from the sky and fell promptly asleep.

    The next day dawned a carbon copy of the previous one, more wind, snow and freezing temperatures. Nothing untoward had happened overnight so after breakfast, I retracted the tent and we set off again. The rest seemed also to have reinvigorated the FPO so it bounced along happily until we got to the ice fields which blanketed the uppermost peaks of the mountain range where its bouncy behaviour was curtailed by the hardness of the ice. Luckily, although I am not great at mountaineering, the route plotted to get to the dome was mostly flat, aside for the final few hundred metres so I fortunately had very little proper climbing to do. On Earth, I hadn't been rich enough to have afforded powered boots which would enable me to fly so I would have to do it the old fashioned way. After a prolonged period of ice hiking, we got to the edge of the ice and then the terrain grew far more rugged. Despite its ability to jump upwards and rotate itself through ninety degrees, the FPO was clearly feeling lazy as it accepted a lift in my warm and comfortable coat pocket.

I soon deployed the crampons which were built into the mountaineering boots. These were essential now as the short slope in front of me was close to vertical and covered in ice. I hefted the ice axe above my head and buried it as far as I could into the ice and began to climb. Progress was slow and difficult and I had several hairy moments when the crampons slipped and I had to cling on for dear life. The FPO didn't seem concerned and poked its prongs out from my pocket and surveyed the ice.

As I got higher up, I risked a quick look over my shoulder - it was obvious that winter was maintaining its grip on the planet as there was ice as far as I could see. Finally, I clambered over the edge, caught my breath and stood on a small promontory to survey the scene. Now at the top, we got an unrivalled view of the landscape. Peering down the other side of the slope, towards the sea, I could see the glistening dome which covered the end of the canyon I'd visited back when the weather was better. Also, in between the breaks in the weather, far in the distance, I saw the spike from the centre of the crater. This was partly buried in snow and ice as well. I switched on the polyscope and used it to peer into the distance. With magnification, I could see that the spike was also swarming with people - perhaps there was enough of the metal visible and extractable even with the thing part buried in snow? I could also see that running directly from the spike to the side of the dome was a magnetised rail system. It occurred to me that the temperature must've been low enough to freeze the ocean. This frozen sea had conveniently provided a perfectly flat surface to build on and they had utilised that to transport the metal to the processing plant which must be in the canyon. My destructive antics previously, much to my annoyance, not really slowed them down much at all. I could also see on the beach that the magnetic pile driving launch system was undergoing construction so at least I could still put a stop to that before the material was launched off into orbit, presumably for collection and transportation to Earth.

On a far more positive note, the way down from the mountain top was much easier especially as I could use the ropes and carabiners that I had brought with me. A few metres of abseiling on a seventy degree slope and I would be on my way down. I threw a good length of rope down into the maelstrom of snow. I could just about see the bottom of the cliff and the instruments built into my helmet told me that it was only twenty metres. However, only twenty metres still seems a long way when you are virtually blinded by snowfall. Nagging at the back of my mind was also the feeling that I couldn't stay up here all day so I checked one last time before launching myself down the slope. The FPO squealed as we rappelled downwards and jumped out from my pocket when we touched down at the bottom of the slope, it clearly really liked the snow. I auto-released the rope which coiled back into its small storage space and then stowed it away in the backpack.

The remainder of the trip down the mountain was much easier. I did toy with the idea of deploying the skis but I'm not a very experienced skier and potentially damaging myself getting down off the slopes did not appeal so I stuck to walking. The wind was less intense on this side of the mountain and the walk wasn't as strenuous as going up. I almost began to enjoy myself as we descended towards the beach. There were plenty of huge rocks scattered about to hide behind in case of being spotted by hostile forces so my progress was measured by a series of zigzags down the mountain.

About half way down, I set up camp for the second night on the mountain. I also found a convenient spot to set up the tent protected from the wind, similar to the previous night. All was peaceful as I dropped off into slumber. However, my sleep was disturbed much later by a massive bombardment of meteors which streaked across the chilly sky, evaporating the clouds with their fireballs and detonating extremely loudly as they impacted on the ice and snow in the distance. I lay awake and, even over the sound of the wind, I heard in the distance, a huge rumbling noise which could only have been an avalanche starting further down the mountain. From the sounds, it appeared to be roughly in the direction of the canyon with the dome at the end of it. A short sleepless while later, the light levels indicated that the suns had risen and the weather had cleared a little. I carefully left the tent and, with the aid of the polyscope, I looked down the mountain to see if there had been any damage. There had. Half the semi completed magnetic launching apparatus had been swept away and the dome was half covered with snow at one side. There was also a massive crack where it had been split by the impact of hundreds of thousands of tonnes of snow. Fortuitously, I now had an entry point.

    I surveilled the operation for a while from my vantage point. The dome appeared to be lightly guarded with minimal security staff and they only seemed interested in the cracked part and not the main gate. Suddenly, there was a loud noise above and behind me and, as I watched, a medium sized ship descended from the clouds. It flew over my position and gradually descended into a perfect landing on the flattish area ahead of the ruined magnetic launch system. As I watched, around twenty individuals exited the rear of the ship and were shepherded towards the opening at the front of the dome. Clearly, these were new recruits to help with the mining. Once through the security perimeter, they spread out and merged into the general throng. Perhaps now would be a good time to go and join in.

    I descended rapidly from my hiding place and headed for the crack in the dome. The guards were now nowhere to be seen so had probably wandered off for a Tealog break or something. The descent of the last few feet was very difficult and I landed awkwardly and twisted my ankle as I reached the crack. Stifling a yell of as a bolt of pain shot up my leg, I noted I was almost down at ground level. At this point, there was only a metre drop to the surface so I let the FPO go first – I wouldn't want to injure the little thing if I landed badly so I commando rolled out off the edge of the ice, somehow landing with most of my weight on my un-sprained left ankle and ending upright at the end of it. Once I'd stopped swearing under my breath at the pain from my leg, I peered around furtively. No one appeared to have seen me. I then retrieved the FPO from the ground and returned it safely to my pocket.

    I noticed to my left a few metres away were a large quantity of bioplastic pallets stacked up so I headed towards those. There was a gap of about a metre between those and the wall of the dome so I had a good place in which to conceal myself. Conscious of the pain in my ankle, I hunkered down, removed my boot and surveyed the damage. It wasn't badly sprained by the look and feel of it so I took the support from the first aid kit and wrapped it round tightly. It would be fine in an hour or so. I straightened up and put my boot on again. The painkillers built into the support were already working so I would be able to walk perfectly well despite the damage. I folded my mountaineering gear away and stowed it outside the dome, through the crack and wondered what to do next.

One other problem that was becoming very apparent was the headache caused by the metal. It had started almost immediately that I had entered the dome area and it was rapidly becoming uncomfortable. I would have to ignore it for now, maybe I would acclimatise in time? As ready as I would ever be, I strolled out into the main operating area of the processing plant. No one else was dressed in uniform aside from the Guardian security staff so I did not stand out. I walked around for a few minutes and must have looked lost because one of the guards approached me.

"You new here?" he asked suspiciously.

"Yep, just arrived on the last transport." I said confidently.

"Had your injections yet?" he asked.

"Nope." I replied while thinking in the confines of my head "What injections?"

"You stupid idiot, you'll be writhing about in agony if you don't get 'em soon. Get to the medical centre, it's over there." He pointed to a large low building a hundred metres away.

"Thanks." I responded. By this point, I was having great difficulty in remaining upright and lucid and was willing to do almost anything to get rid of the pain pulsating through my brain. As I lurched off toward the medical block, I heard him mutter something about "stupid civilian yonks" but I ignored him and walked away.

The building was just like any hospital back on Earth. The corridors smelled of Iodoform and were painted uniform neutral colours. I headed to the front desk where a group of people were milling about while a nurse fussed over them trying to organise where they were supposed to go. She smiled for a fraction of a second when I walked in and then continued to deal with the others. Once they had all gone, she asked me what I needed. I replied I'd come for my new arrivals injections. She sighed heavily and pointed down the long central corridor.

"First door on the left, marked Newbies," she said curtly.

"Thanks." I replied and followed her instructions.

The room was about five metres squared and comprised of a single desk, with another nurse sat on an uncomfortable looking chair behind it and a rack of trays, each with a syringe like device in it.

"Next," she said in a bored fashion. I approached the desk.

"New?" she asked.

"Yes, just arrived on the last transport," I replied.

"Arm," she said efficiently.

I rolled up my sleeve and presented her with my left arm. She held the syringe against the inside of my elbow and depressed the button at the far end. There was a faint sound like the exhaling of a small animal and that was it. Almost immediately, I felt far better than I had done since returning to Ventos. I flexed my arm muscles, mumbled my thanks and marched out of the room with a clearer head than I had done in several hours. The nurse did not look up and scribbled away on a piece of rewritable paper which was on her left.

I looked around the hospital, there was no security here so, for now, I was safe. Strolling further down the corridor I noticed an unmarked door. Glancing round casually to see that no one was watching me, I gripped the handle and opened it. It was a cleaning cupboard. All around the walls were assorted cleaning apparatus and bottles of disinfectant. It stank so I turned around and made my way out as quickly as I could. I walked a short distance down the corridor. There were doors on either side, presumably leading to wards for any injured workers and maybe storage rooms for medical supplies. I decided it was best to leave everything alone and make my exit.

    I left the medical block and marched back across the main open area. I decided to have a little reconnoitre of the complex. The main processing plant was in the centre of the dome, it was a large ugly building with one very tall storey and some large pipes which connected to the protective perimeter of the dome. Smoke and fumes were clearly vented outside rather than letting them build up inside and poisoning everyone within it. No one challenged me as everyone in the whole place seemed to be in a perpetual state of chaos with people running around. Some of them were clutching large sheaves of rewritable paper and others had followers in tow, full of the metallic substance and equipment.

    The processing plant was vast. The echoes from the sounds generated by the workforce within were deafening so I pilfered a set of ear defenders from the pegs by the door. That was much better, I could at least now hear myself think. A small booth on my left was clearly a break area as it contained tea and coffee analogue generation equipment and some card operated vending machines. I was feeling a little peckish so entered the room. There was no one else in there so I made myself a free cup of Tealog and sat down for a few minutes. Unfortunately, I couldn't buy any food as I didn't have any cards to pay for it. I did still have supplies in my pockets so I fished out a chocolate bar and ate that. Physically, I felt better than I had done for ages however, my mind was awash with panic and planning. After a brief and much needed stop in the other booth on the right hand side, I decided to have a proper look around.

    I walked around the rectangular perimeter; the whole thing was basically one big open space with a conveyer belt running from one side to the other. The new ore arrived in at the left hand entry point via a two track monorail from the spike and exited at the opposite side. I could see clearly that one track was for giant followers, full of rock and the other side was for passengers - in this case the miners who were extracting the material. Once within the confines of the dome, the first area which the ore went through was a laboratory, replete with people in lab coats who were sticking probes into the metal as it trundled very slowly by. Every so often one of them would grab a test tube full, dissolve it up in some liquid and then put it into what looked like a desktop mass spectrometer which was presumably for determining the purity of the ore. All around were the usual things you find in labs, balances, particle accelerators, pipettes and really, really uncomfortable looking chairs. There were other assorted equipment which, despite my scientific training, I was unable to recognise. A faint solvent smell also permeated all around this area. This part of the structure was isolated from the remainder of the building by a transparent wall.

The next section involved people and machines hefting quantities of the ore off the conveyer and feeding them into a large machine, shaped like a giant turbine. It whirled around and the ore passed out the other end, presumably purified to the correct level based upon readings from the laboratory section and was then heaved back onto the conveyer by another group of workers and a few fairly rubbish looking robots. The final part of the operation consisted of a packing plant, where the material was partitioned into innocuous looking bioplastic crates before being fed out of the exit door on the other side. I walked past all of this activity, all the while trying to figure out a way to stop it permanently with the minimum of fuss and without injuring anyone. Probably the safest thing to do would be to interrupt the conveyer before it got to the laboratory. The only problem was I hadn't seen the apparatus properly to get any ideas on how to do this but it seemed sensible to stop it there before it got too far along. It occurred to me that if needs be, I could also sabotage the packaging part, just to make doubly sure.

Just after the packing plant was a small section of the conveyer which was unattended. I walked past a small desk which had on it a set of bioplastic clipboards and rewritable paper so I grabbed one, put on my most serious inspector face and headed towards the belt. It was a typical twenty third century ionic flow conveyer, nothing fancy or difficult to understand. Basically, the lower part of the device was positively charged and the actual conveyer was fluid based and consisted of a negatively charged membrane which was repelled from the positively charged lower level. An electric current induced a flow of particles from one end to the other so that it moved. Speed could be altered by increasing or decreasing the amount of electrical charge which was applied. Disrupting it would be simple – all I needed to do was interrupt or disrupt the flow of electricity to the membrane. The control module was actually at this end so this would be a good place to sabotage it from. If I could disturb the conveyer in three places simultaneously, I should be able to put it out of action for a long period of time. This would cause the membrane to totally loose its ability to conduct charge and need to be completely rebuilt and repolarised. I looked around for something to do this with. There was nothing available that could be used to disrupt it nearby but in my backpack I had some lengths of superconducting filaments. One of these wrapped around the lower section would do the trick. I also had several portable batteries which could be used to generate the necessary charge in the fibre or alternatively, I could connect it into the mains power supply. Either way, I had the beginnings of a plan.

The Ventos Conspiracy 2

     I put the clipboard back on the table as I wandered past and headed out of the building smiling slightly, now intent on returning to my hiding place. Trying to fit in with the other workers was fine when they were working but sneaking into a sleeping area and trying to hide there would be extremely foolhardy so the best plan was to set up camp just outside the dome near the crack. There was heat leakage from the structure so at least just outside would be slightly warmer than it would be than if I was isolated from it by a large distance. It was late afternoon by now so making arrangements for sleeping would be a good idea. I also still had plenty of rations left so eating wasn't a problem. As for other concerns, I could always pop back inside and use the right hand room when needed.

     The FPO had remained very quiet while I had wondered about the place but now it was growing restive. I now made my way to the area behind the pallets, put on my cold weather gear again and climbed out through the crack and onto the ice. As the dome was mostly transparent, sneaking along the edge of it would be impossible so I clambered straight up the ice face and back into the avalanche debris and kept climbing. The slope wasn't too bad and I made quick progress to a relatively flat area which contained a large boulder that shielded my position from anyone who may have been looking out of the dome. I then dug a snow tunnel by means of a couple of carefully aimed blasts of the mining laser so I had a hole to sleep in. I climbed in, ate my dinner and watched the FPO have a play in the snow. By now I had a good plan of how to stop this part of the operation but no idea how to stop the main operation at the central spike. I would go and have a look at that in the morning so I settled into my sleeping bag and drifted off to sleep.

It was quite snug in my little ice-hole and I awoke naturally the following morning when the light levels were just about passable. I had slept well as there had not been any meteors overnight for a change. Sticking my head out from the chamber I noticed that the snow was a little less intense this morning, meaning improved visibility. I struggled out of my sleeping bag, dressed quickly and left my hidey hole. Walking carefully up to the rock, I peered around the corner towards the dome. Interestingly, work had not really started yet – in all my time there I had never heard any alarms alerting people that it was time to have a break or start their shifts which seemed strange. Such things were commonplace on Earth so why not here? I watched for a few minutes and despite the lack of a signal, the workforce emerged from the buildings on the right hand side which must have been the sleeping areas. A few of them were stretching and clearly having conversations but most of them seemed to be remarkably obedient. A couple of Guardians loitered about, watching them disinterestedly as they filed into the main processing plant.

The Ventos Conspiracy 2

     I needed to get on the monorail to get to the central spike so I circled around the dome staying within the confines of the ice until the point that the outflow from the avalanche stopped. Unlike my chosen entry point for the entrance to the crack, here it gently sloped down to ground level so I walked in without the need for any heroics.

     I walked confidently round to the entrance to the monorail which was at the front of the dome, facing out towards the frozen sea and facing the spike. Glancing secretively at the apparatus, it looked as if it worked in the same fashion as the ionic conveyer so could be disrupted in the same way. As elsewhere, security was light so it was simple to mingle with a group of workers and be hoarded onto the train. In due course, the train sped off from the terminus and took all of five minutes to get to the spike. The surface of the frozen ocean was lumpy, but generally featureless ice. While I travelled, I sat and pondered this strange way of building a train. When I thought about it, it seemed logical as the ice might not be terribly thick so it would be easier to construct an ionic flow system which would weigh a lot less than a solid track. The train would float above the membrane and not put any weight on the ice, all of which also made it far easier to disrupt.

A short while later we disembarked *en masse* onto the slopes which led up to the spike. I looked up. From here, it looked impossibly high and, when the sun broke through the snowy clouds, it glinted evilly. The actual mining operation was concentrated on the side of the spike facing the coast so I followed the herd of workers to the entrance. They said little as they slowly progressed around in a group. I noted that several of them looked haggard and had a strange look in their eyes as if they weren't really sure what they were doing.

There were three buildings near the entrance, a food hall, a toilet block and another smaller structure which could have been an engineering store or similar. It appeared that thus far, all the metal they'd extracted must have come from here as the volumes required to make everyone wear a bracelet or necklace, even on the planet with a much reduced population, would be enormous. There were several of the large mining vehicles like the one I'd blown up previously and with these, members of the workforce were driving into the hole and blasting away the rock. Others then scuttled in and collected the ore onto the giant followers. These were then directed to the monorail track for transportation to the mainland and purification in the processing plant.

The entrance to the newly created cave was bolstered with large metal mining props to prevent the whole thing from collapsing. I thought for a minute and decided that maybe these could be "removed" to collapse the mine. It did seem a rather silly way of mining this deposit as the metal mountain would be inherently unstable and, with the strong gusty winds, it was possible that the whole thing might blow over anyway. At a guess, I assumed that the plan was actually to collapse it so it was facing towards the coast and therefore make the mining simpler. Obviously, before they did that they would have to ascertain that the ice was thick enough to take the weight. However, if the spike could be persuaded to fall the other way, out to sea where the ice was presumably less thick, then it would crash though and be lost in the depths of the ocean – provided it was heavy enough to break the ice, of course. My earlier experiments with the material had shown it to be very dense and heavy therefore I surmised this would seem a likely result. My only problem with this plan would be making sure that the workers were clear of the structure when it went over. I had no wish to harm innocent bystanders who were merely following orders, perhaps without even knowing it. This ruled out a mission during daylight when I could easily be spotted. Night time would definitely be the best for avoiding casualties and also detection. I spent another couple of hours scouting around the mine, trying to look busy and frequently grabbing piles of rewritable paper to blend in with the hundreds of folk working away diligently. I noted that security was light so after a useful few hours, I joined a group of workers on the monorail back to the main complex and the dome.

Once back inside, I sneaked round to the crack and made my way back towards my snow hole. All this time, the FPO had remained silent but it was beginning to get irritable and so once back at my camp, I let it play in the snow for a while. It didn't seem to be itself at the moment, it was either absolutely manic or very quiet. Perhaps it was tired as the UV lamp I had brought with me was not as powerful as the one on the ship. Unfortunately, the amount of things I could carry was limited and so this was an unfortunate side effect.

Another thing I had noticed in my short time back on the planet was the skies did seem a little clearer now so perhaps the weather was breaking and the icy grip was beginning to loosen. This was unfortunate as it meant I perhaps only had a short time to complete my destruction of the mining operation with a reasonable probability of evading capture, due to the snow and ice. On the other hand, the ice would also be melting so perhaps the excavation was in danger due to the same reason, I had no way of telling. Once back in my snow hollow, I made the usual preparations and went to sleep.

The next day dawned even clearer than the last. I could almost hear the snow melting which could prove bothersome if my tracks became visible. Pale watery sunlight from the suns was shining through the entrance of the tent when I awoke. Due to the vast amount of ice, it would persist for some time but I need to complete my mission as quickly and efficiently as possible. Thinking logically, there were advantages to the thaw, it could mean my tracks in the snow would be destroyed as things melted and it also meant the FPO could feed properly. I looked over at the poor little green animal and then decided to let it out to play for a while before I made my way back to the dome. After that, it seemed a little happier and squeaked at me for the first time in a few days.

I checked my knapsack to see if I still had some superconducting filament, a couple of spare battery packs and some timers so that I could disable the ionic conveyers in the way that I had envisaged. Fortunately, all were still present and had not been stolen by The Union security personnel during my incarceration and torture.

I sneaked round the dome in the usual manner but noticed that something was different. There were far more people around and more of the characteristically dressed Guardians were visible. Until now, I had not seen many of them so a transport must have arrived overnight. There were maybe half a dozen clothed in their distinctive sea blue coloured suits with green ties (the suit representing the sea, the tie the land). They were pointing at things and generally being officious, just like back on Earth. I noted with horror that there was one of them directing a group of surly looking workers to repair the crack in the dome so my usual method of getting in and out might not be accessible for much longer.

     I moved further back onto the avalanche debris and crept around as far as was possible and, when no one seemed to be looking, I joined a throng of workers being berated by a tall blue suited man with an unpleasant face. Once in the group, I felt safer and I let myself be herded into the dome. I split off from the main group with another two people and we trudged into the main processing area. As I walked in, I swiped a bioplastic clipboard and headed for the lab. I had decided the best way to blend in was to conduct my sabotage from in there as it was always busy and, having worked in a lab for a while, I would be able to make it look like I knew what I was doing.

     I entered the transparent room without fuss, there were no Guardians in here. As on Earth, the life expectancy for analysts was always slightly lower due to exposure to dangerous chemicals so perhaps that was why none of them dared to come in here. As I grabbed a visitor's lab coat from the rack on the wall, I nodded at the other analysts who were busying themselves with analysis and entering data into the computer terminals. I was just heading for the corner of the room where the conveyer was when I was jostled by another analyst who dropped her one hundred millilitre volumetric flask on the floor.

"Aw, hi, erm, shit, sorry about that!" I said and bent down to help her retrieve the broken shards of glass.

"No matter." she replied curtly and continued to pick up the bits. Then she tutted and said:

"Don't do that without gloves, you idiot, you'll cut yourself!"

She shooed me out of the way and headed to a sharps bin on a nearby bench and dropped the shards in. Then she wondered off to get another flask from a cupboard on the far side of the lab. I watched her go. She was about my age, slim, pretty and petite with a neat light brown bob haircut and an air of fierce intelligence about her. As I turned to go I felt her looking at me so I turned round and looked at her. As our eyes met, I felt the characteristic flutter in my stomach which could only mean one thing. In the confines of my head my brain screamed at me while I smiled weakly and left the area, giving her a little wave as I walked out.

Once out of the central part of the lab and out of sight from the analysts, I set about my task, all the time trying not to think about her. I made my way quickly to the end of the conveyor. It was surprisingly easy to wrap the cable around the membrane, connect both ends into the back of the battery pack and then set a timer. After much pondering, I decided to set it to go off in the middle of the following night. Security was light and the chances of them discovering all three devices, once they were in place, was minimal. As I was leaving, I glanced around in the direction of the lab for the young woman, she was over in the corner by a bench, expertly filling up assorted volumetric flasks with solvents. I reluctantly took my eyes off her and headed for the outer door. Hanging up my labcoat, I looked back across at her wistfully one last time, just as she glanced in my direction. Our eyes met for a second, she smiled, I blushed and then she busied herself with her task and I very reluctantly walked off.

  I then proceeded to the middle part of the conveyer, the bit where people were hefting ore about. This was unusually deserted today and so in less than five minutes, that part of my mission was completed. The packaging section was a little more difficult, this was swarming with people. As I approached the edge of the dome, in the distance I could see another ship coming in to land on the now partially reconstructed airstrip on the beach. Although the snow was less intense today, there was still a fair covering and landing crews were struggling to keep it clear. This particular ship was far larger and more impressive than any that I had seen so far and it proudly displayed The Union logo on the outside (as if anyone in space cared whether it was on display or not).

It was also accompanied by a much smaller, beleaguered looking craft which clearly looked as though it had been in the wars as the outside was scorched and melted. Somehow I knew it was the ship I'd helped crash on the dead Earth in the Bok globule. Both ships were close to the ground now and would touchdown shortly so I hung back at the entrance to the dome waiting for them to land. They landed and as I looked on, the blue uniformed Guardians formed a neat line either side of the exit ramp and a short woman with mad frizzy greying hair descended to ground level. As I was out of earshot, I was unable to hear any of the ensuing conversation but it was clear she must be a dignitary of some description. I thought hard for a minute, and something niggled at the back of my mind - this could be the mythical Stella Nivos, the supposed female head of The Union. I watched as she strode along the already re-freezing landing strip and disappeared onto the monorail, presumably for some sort of tour. The remainder of my sabotage would have to wait a while as security would be beefed up by the presence of such an important figure. As I watched, the other ship also emptied of occupants, namely Scarface, an angry looking thin woman, who might have been Townsend, and the worried looking older man. They had survived the crash but it had taken them a while to repair the ship after their nosedive onto the planet. They had presumably been intercepted by the main ship to act as a security detail as it passed through the Bok globule.

If I'd known this was going to happen, I would have planned it differently. Triggering my devices on the ionic conveyer in the processing plant would be insane at this time but they were on a timer so I had no option but to let them go off. The best plan would be to return to my hiding place and wait until things had gone quiet again. I estimated it would take them a couple days to realign the ionic flow in the conveyer so at least that should hold them up for a while. Another problem was with the several weeks journey to and from Ventos. The dignitaries would have to be here for some time in order to make their visit worthwhile and all this time, the ice was melting increasing my chances of discovery. In order to carry out my plan, I would need to be very, very careful in sabotaging the spike mining operation and the monorail.

I couldn't sleep that night, I was too occupied pondering how to get around this situation. If only the dignitaries hadn't hoved into view at that point, my plan might well have succeeded in one fell swoop. As I tried to doze off, meteors began to rain down on the planet scuppering any chance of a decent night's sleep. In that weird, semi-conscious state my mind wandered from one scenario to the other and back again, many of them involving the young woman from the lab. By the middle of the night I was again wide awake and thinking far too clearly to go back to sleep. In my sleep deprived state, it dawned on me that I had a fantastic opportunity to take down the whole operation and that I was being unnecessarily cautious. There was still a while until the timers went off so maybe it was time for action.

The Ventos Conspiracy 2

Chapter two – Chrysanthemum

At some point equivalent to around five in the morning, while it was still dark and the meteors were still sporadically falling, I decided to head back to the ship. After all, it was a converted mining ship so I could sneak through the defences and blow the absolute shit out of the spike using the mining lasers. The ship had the necessary sensors and equipment to detect where the weakest point on the spike was so that my attack should be completely successful. So, at first light, even though I was exhausted from a sleepless night, I set off. It would take a couple of days for me to get back to *The Cowrie* and by then, the conveyer would be disabled and I would be clear of anyone looking for a saboteur. Then, just as they were starting to affect repairs, they would receive another hopefully even more massive much larger setback.

I set off, FPO in tow, back over the mountains. We made rapid progress by tracking up the avalanche which, by now had set solid and so was much safer to walk on. The weather did seem to be steadily improving and so we made rapid progress away from the dome. Within a few hours I was back in the ice fields and heading for the peaks. Now with the better visibility, even without the navigational system, I could easily see other routes which would avoid the need for abseiling or climbing so there were no periods of time when I was not on the move. As before, at nightfall, I set up the tent in the lee of another gigantic boulder.

I awoke in the middle of the night in a cold sweat. From this distance, it was absolutely impossible for me to have heard anything from the dome but I was certain I had. I grabbed my portable laser and opened the entrance to the tent and peered out into the freezing darkness. There was absolutely nothing except kilometres and kilometres of ice in all directions. The snow had started up again and it was coming down thick and fast, deadening any noises there might have been. This was not really a surprise as I was significantly higher up in the mountains. The sound I heard must have been my imagination so I disappeared back into the tent and somehow or other managed to doze off again.

At first light, the scene was much the same, only slightly snowier. I had maybe a solid days trekking to get to the ship so I set off as quickly as I could with the FPO playing silly games in the snow, just like before. I did note that it seemed a little more tired these days, a bit less willing to play and it appeared somehow to look angrier than it used to. Of course, I had no idea how long the life span was, maybe they only lived for a year or maybe the cold conditions and lack of light were beginning to have a deleterious effect on it? I hoped that maybe once back on the ship and under the UV, it would regain its former vigour. Just after lunch, it had tired sufficiently that I scooped it up and put it back into my long overcoat pocket where it rested comfortably in the warmth. I'd grown really attached to the little thing over the last few months and it had saved my life several times. However I was aware that it perhaps had a tribe or family and it was a long way away from them. Perhaps it might be time to return to the house as well and see if that would cheer it up. However, my first priority was to stop The Union so we trudged on through the freezing environment, now heading down the slope of the mountain to where I had secured the ship.

It was hard to spot her amongst the snow and the increasing darkness but once I got close, it was obvious. I activated the external ramp and clambered back on board. The first thing I did was put the FPO back in its little dirt box and flick the UV lamp onto full power. It seemed to like this and almost purred as it warmed up and settled. Then I had a hot shower and changed my clothes. It was pitch dark now outside and so probably the best time to set off and destroy the spike. Despite the now worsening weather, the ship was only slightly more buried than it had been when I left and what there was no problem clearing it as the snow was fresh and soft. Within seconds of becoming airborne, I had covered the distance that had taken us two whole days of solid hiking to traverse. I flew over the top of the mountains and slowed to a crawl. The whole place was a mess – even from here I could see that it was swarming with people and the Guardians were far more obvious than they had been before. I had clearly made the right choice in running away for I would surely have been spotted if I'd stayed put.

    I flew carefully across the last section of the wasteland below, trying not to disturb the freshly fallen snow. Instead of turning left to go toward the complex and the dome, I turned right, heading around the perimeter of the crater ocean. I flew on for around ten minutes, keeping an eye open for any pursuing craft but there was nothing on the scanners. Once I judged I had gone far enough, I flew across the frozen ocean on an intercept course with the spike. To my naked unassisted eyes, it barely showed up in the darkness but the night vision sensors had no bother in picking it up. I held my position five hundred metres from it at a height of a couple of metres from the surface of the frozen sea. The mining scanners would take approximately one minute to complete their analysis of where the weakest point in the structure was but once this was done I could fire the main mining lasers. Following that, my position would be visible to all and sundry so it was imperative that once I'd fired and the spike was collapsing, I hit the main engines and got off the planet.

    It was a tense minute while the computers crunched the numbers. There was no activity on the scanners and no sign of anyone within range. The tension was broken by an attention grabbing noise as the computer display informed me of the structurally worst spot to fire at, as it would cause a collapse. I noted this, flicked off the camo drive and fired all the main mining lasers and the augmented weapons systems at that one spot.

     Several bright streaks of pretty blue light shot across the ice, reflecting attractively on the opaque surface as they covered the intervening distance from the gun barrel to the spike in mere fractions of a second. The secondary weapons systems then launched their barrage, a few milliseconds later. The computer had said it would take a concentrated ten second burst from the main lasers to destroy the weakest part of the structure and the props so I kept my finger hard on the firing button. Five seconds in, sensors detected that a ship had launched from the base, accompanied by three of the smaller remote scout ships. I held my nerve and my finger... The metal began to melt and flow and a hole began to appear in the side of the spike. I could almost hear it creaking and seven seconds in it began to lean dangerously towards me...
Eight seconds...
Nine seconds and a blast of laser fire from one of the ships missed me by a couple of metres...
Ten seconds, the whole internal support wall of the thing melted and the spike listed slightly towards me. As I hung there in the air watching, I fired off a couple

additional shots at the remaining struts supporting the opening of the mine. Then the spike began to move far more quickly, plunging towards me. On the way down, it caught the wing of the larger ship, sending it spinning into the ice. *The Cowrie*'s main engines fired just as the camo drive activated and I blasted upwards into the atmosphere. At the same time, the enormous weight of the spike smashed through the surface of the sea ice sending up huge columns of water and tectonic plate sized chunks of ice into the air. Then, silently, I watched in the rear view camera as it sank like a stone. I recorded this so I could watch it later but I allowed myself a self-congratulatory gesture as I exited the planet's atmosphere. I also saw, when re-watching my recording later that a huge chrysanthemum of flame had shot out from the stump of the decapitated spike and incinerated everything in its path, including the three remaining scout ships.

Sadly, according to the scanners, I discovered that I had a major problem - within seconds of the explosion, another three scout ships had been launched. They were accompanied by the bigger ship in which the visiting dignitary had arrived. It was now going to be a case of trying to lose them in the interplanetary space between here and Earth. Trouble was, they would easily guess that I was headed there so a less than friendly reception committee would be waiting for me when I arrived. I had planned to return to Earth to deal with the remainder of

The Union but if they were expecting me, it would be even more difficult. This meant somehow I needed to cripple all the ships following me in order to prevent them from transmitting a warning to Earth. Between here and the other side of the Bok globule, I needed to deal with them. I powered the engines up to maximum and blasted out of orbit, heading straight to the Bok globule. Unfortunately, within a couple of minutes, all four ships were on my tail. A warning light on the main panel informed me that they had opened up a communication channel as soon as they were within range:

"Stand down and prepare to be boarded!" buzzed the intercom with a familiar dulcet tone.

"Paul Francis Heath, you are wanted for crimes against The Union. Stand down or we'll shoot you down!" barked Scarface angrily.

"Sorry old pal," I retorted, "can't do that. By the way, it's Franz, not Francis."

I slammed the ship into a steep dive just as a laser flashed through the space I had previously occupied.

I fired the rear laser cannons back at them but missed by a fair margin as they banked sharply out of the way. I then executed a barrel roll as they fired again and again. Each time they were getting closer and I was taking more and more risks. The courses in the ice cavern had been good but hadn't really prepared me for this so I had to learn fast. I levelled off for a second and then banked steeply and pulled up on the controls hard and came up behind one of the smaller ships. I launched one of the smaller missiles and grinned as the engines exploded and the ship spun off in a flat spin. One down, three to go.

Scarface now appeared in person on the viewscreen looking even more annoyed than before.
"Last chance you fuckin' Johnson!" he said and launched another missile. One of things I'd learnt on the tactical avoidance courses was fire while they are firing at you so a nice blast of blue laser light destroyed the missile in mid-flight. Another blast milliseconds after hit the cockpit of the ship right in front of me, that had been on an approach vector. Two down...

Ship number three belonged to Scarface who was clearly a very accomplished pilot. As we screamed across the void of space, time and again he fired at me and it was more by luck than good judgement that he missed. Finally, after a very close shave where he destroyed a non-essential part of the wing, causing a distinct wobble in my flight, I did a seemingly stupid thing and turned off the engines completely. I was close to the second planet in the system at the time and so fell under its gravitational influence. The ship began to spiral unpredictably into the atmosphere of the probably uninhabited planet and Scarface followed plunging headfirst down into the increasingly thick atmosphere.

He fired once or twice but as my course was so erratic, he missed. As I descended through the cloud layer, the red collision alert warning lights began to flash urgently. At the very last second, I turned the engines back on and shot back up into the atmosphere. After a few seconds of rapid climbing, I pointed the nose of *The Cowrie* downwards so I was facing the top part of his ship. Once within range, I fired all of the lasers at it. Direct hit! It didn't stand a chance as the left hand wing was severed from the fuselage and the ship went down in a steep spiral and exploded on the surface in an impressive orange cloud. I yelled some self-congratulatory words, cursed Scarface to a very painful eternity in oblivion and then looked around for the other larger ship.

While all this had been going on, the main ship had used the opportunity to put some distance between me and it and was clearly headed for the globule and Earth. They were getting away but their ship was very much larger and bulkier than mine and so I figured that I should be able to catch them at maximum thrust. It wouldn't hurt to go a little faster so using the planet I had narrowly escaped crashing on as a gravitational slingshot, I accelerated past the red line on the engine output display and literally blasted clear of the atmosphere and off in pursuit.

In order to get to the Bok globule, it was necessary to fly towards the twin suns. As I followed the enemy ship's course on the scanners, I noticed that it took a detour to avoid the left of the two suns. Therefore, if I wanted to catch them even more quickly, the best thing to do would be to plot a course right between the two stars. They were separated by several tens of millions of kilometres so there was no danger of being fried however the gravitational forces might make for an interesting flight. I didn't have long to ponder this so I set a course.

The engines were whining loudly as I streaked towards the two flaming orbs. Within seconds I had passed the first planet in the system, a tiny, uninhabitable ball of rock smaller than Mercury in size. It was too close to the stars to support life and surface temperatures would have been in excess of 1000°C during the day. The scans told me there were also abundant volcanoes and lava flows which covered the surface. As I whizzed past, it occurred to me that in the course of the fight, I had drained the solar batteries so this would be a good opportunity to recharge the cells as well. I opened up the covers and let the solar energy flow directly into the rechargeable cells. Within a few minutes, the ship was back up to full power for the first time in ages. It also replenished the batteries for every single on-board system and subsystem.

As I approached the suns, it became apparent that it was going to take all my strength to hold a straight course due to the tidal gravitational forces between them. I began to sweat as the temperature increased and as I struggled to hold the joystick steady. The ship began to rattle and I valiantly held on. Suddenly, an overhead relay exploded and showered me with hot water. I wiped the moisture from my eyes and hung on like grim death.

"Come on, come on!" I muttered under my breath as the suns grew larger on the screen in front of me. Just as I reached the point equidistant between the two suns, the wobbling ceased and there was a few seconds of calm, like the eye of a storm. I'd not been watching the enemy ship and now, as I had time and wasn't struggling to hold course, I risked a look at the long range scanner. I was definitely gaining on them and I was probably shielded from their sensors by the intense solar radiation so it was a win on both counts. As suddenly as it had ceased, the wobbling started again and I tightened my grip on the joystick. This continued for perhaps another five minutes while I struggled to be free of the immense tidal gravity forces.

There was a loud sound from the bow of the ship as I escaped the last of the sun's gravitational effects. Whatever had happened, it had not affected my trajectory or speed so I carried on regardless. I was now almost within weapons range of the larger ship and it was only at this short distance that I realised how huge the vessel was. I was at least twenty times bigger than *The Cowrie* and was horribly beweaponed. I fired a shot across the bow, missed and in return, a railgun popped out of a bulkhead and returned fire. The ensuing volley of projectiles hit the ship several times and a few lights and alarms went off but I ignored them. I was still gaining but the systems were now objecting wildly to being pushed this hard. I really needed to stop and effect some repairs or else I would be in serious trouble. Suddenly, the ship in front slowed appreciably and so I launched what proved to be a totally ineffective attack on the engines. In return, more railguns appeared and fired back. Because of the volume of the barrage, it was impossible to avoid them all and my ship took several hits including a what sounded like a bad one to the engines. Despite the inertia from my slingshot, the impacts altered my course and then another larger volley of bullets took out navigational controls and main weapons. The ship began to spiral off course and despite my best efforts, I could not maintain my pursuit. After a profuse bout of swearing, I realised I was in serious trouble. Instead of zooming off into the darkness leaving me to die in the blackness of space, The Union ship came to a full stop ahead of me and fired a grappling hook at the hull. There was a shudder as it dug its claws into the metal plating. I was then slowly wound in towards the larger ship and within a couple of minutes, I was drawn into one of the massive hangar bays.

The Ventos Conspiracy 2

I sat still, not sure what to do. I looked around for inspiration but nothing came to mind. I didn't panic, I would no doubt have ample time for that later on. I walked over to the dirt box and looked at the FPO, it was buried deeply in the debris and seemed unconcerned by all the explosions, acrid smoke and mayhem. I reached down and patted it gently. It looked up at me and squeaked back questioningly at me. We obviously couldn't communicate in any meaningful way but we'd got used to each other's presence over the last few months and become sort of friends. I'd spent hours talking to it when we'd been lost in the tunnels and in the ice chamber and I'd really grown very fond of it. It had been my only friend in the lonely and isolated situation I had put myself in. The Union were well known for their lack of tolerance of traitors and for making people disappear so I was probably going to end up dead, alone in the darkness. I thought fleetingly of the girl in the lab and of my family, of the silly songs we used to make up in moments of boredom. All the time I'd been on Ventos, I had not really thought about them but suddenly, they all seemed rather important. I felt tears welling up in the corners of my eyes.

I was shaken out of my misery by the FPO which squeaked insistently at me just as there was a tremendous knocking on the door of the ship. I sniffed, wiped my eyes with the backs of my hands and put the

FPO back carefully in the dirt box, there was no telling what they would do to it if they found it.

"Open up now or we'll blast the door open!" came a loud and officious sounding voice.

I sniffed again, stood up slowly and looked around wearily. I had no choice but to let them in. The ship was a bit battered already and losing the main hatch would not help at all. I crossed over to the door and released the airlock mechanism. There was the obligatory whoosh sound as the air pressures equalised and I was met with half a dozen mean looking people all dressed in blue suits. This time, I was clearly getting special treatment as a group of Guardians had come to knock on my door.

"Mr. Heath," said the one at the front levelly, "we meet at last."

Then he punched me in the stomach and I fell to the ground.

He stood over me and spoke menacingly:

"You've destroyed several ships and drones and taken out our mining operation on Ventos. Why the fuck did you do that?" he asked and kicked me in the stomach.

"Do you have a problem with us?" another kick.

"Do you have some sense of misplaced loyalty to the human race?" Another kick.

I drew breath and wheezed back:

"Perhaps if you stopped kicking me in the stomach I might be able to answer you properly!"

With this, he threw back his head and laughed, a proper pantomime villain laugh with no actual humour involved whatsoever.

"Oh, I see, a fuckin' comedian." He said and kicked me again.

"Take him to the cells!"

I was hauled bodily to my feet and dragged off down the corridor. I wasn't able to determine much but I was taken down a long passageway, gun metal grey and through a veritable maze of passages, ending up in a dank and dark hallway which smelled horrible. The door buzzed open automatically when the guard on the left held his hand up to it and I was thrown unceremoniously inside.

The cell was about three metres square, grey in colour and had no distinguishing features whatsoever aside from a control panel on the left hand side. There was a primitive looking toilet in the corner, a washbasin and a very thick hessian floor covering at one side of the cell which presumably was supposed to be a bed. It didn't look very homely at all. There was a single uncomfortable looking chair and a lean to table set up on the right hand side of the cell and a plain looking clock set into the wall, presumably so you could measure how long you'd been in the cell all on your own. The lights were barely on and the whole place exuded an atmosphere of misery. I staggered to my feet and made my way over to the chair and sat down, nursing my aching ribs. Luckily, this time they didn't feel like they were broken. In all my clever planning, I had not anticipated this happening and so now I was stumped as to how to escape and prevent the coming cataclysm on Earth. At least the FPO was safe on the ship – it seemed intelligent enough to hide when in danger so it should be able to stay out of trouble and look after itself. As I sat there, everything seemed desperate, all alone, locked in a metal cell and at the mercy of my enemies. Even with my eternal optimism, I couldn't see a way out. I just wondered how long it would be before they came along and tortured me or whatever else they had in mind. Even the grim thought that The Union were rumoured to pump a gas into their prison cells which contained a compound derived from rare species of jellyfish that created a sense of unease didn't help to lift my mood. I cursed my stupidity at having gone after the larger and heavily armed ship in the first place.

  I didn't have long to wait for company. I'd sat there for about ten minutes catching my breath and mentally beating myself up when the door popped open and in marched the same two Guardians as before along with a different commanding officer.
  "Get up!" the man in charge snarled.

  I did and then I was once again hauled bodily down the corridors. A few moments later, we reached a large chamber set up like a courtroom. I was directed to an area which was isolated from the remainder of the room by a spike topped partition. There were four people present including me. The senior looking man made his way up to a raised chair at one end of the room and made himself comfortable. I sat down on a rickety plastic looking chair, flanked by two Guardians.

"Right", he said, shifting himself in his comfy looking chair and looking very smug.
"You, Mr. Paul Francis Heath, are being charged with treason against The Union, destruction of Union property, murder, conspiracy, terrorism, sedition and theft. You are guilty on all charges and the punishment for these crimes is death. We don't want to do that out here in space, we want to make an example of you so we're going to hold a full trial back on Earth and beam it across The Network for all to see. Your death will serve as a warning to others. Do you have anything to say?"

"Yes," I replied angrily rising to my feet and shaking my fist at him "For the last time, you cloth eared Johnson, my middle name is Franz! My parents were obsessed with Franz Schubert and so gave me a middle name in honour of him. It would be nice if, as I'm being sentenced to death, that you could at least get my bloody name right!"

The officer looked at me coldly for a while, peering over his glasses. He coughed slightly and said, perhaps a little too loudly, "Take him back to his cell. Please."

I was then dragged out of the enclosure and returned to my cell. At least I knew what was going to happen and by my estimations, I had about three weeks left to live. Three weeks to plan how to get out of here and save the Earth. I felt utterly miserable and alone.

The next few days blurred into one. The light levels in the cell were dimmed to simulate night and day but most of the time, it was just dull. I was completely alone with my thoughts and the only people I saw were those who delivered my meagre meals. They didn't talk to me much except to insult me from time to time over the intercom and through the hole in the door which the meals were delivered through. I kept myself physically busy by doing light exercises but aside from that, I had absolutely nothing to do. At least if I was fit and healthy, I might be able to escape if there was a chance to do so. However, my mind was whirling around, looking for scenarios in which I might be able to affect an escape but despite my best efforts, I could not think of any way I might be able to. Even if I was able to incapacitate one of the guards, the other would no doubt be able to stop me and, even if I could escape from the cell, where would I go? I was on a ship in deep space. I often wondered if the FPO was ok but decided that presumably it could take care of itself.

On the seventh day, I awoke as usual when the light levels in the cell were increased. The clock read 07:00. A few moments later a guard opened the hole in the cell door in the usual fashion and placed the tray on the hatch. I took a couple of steps forward to grab my tray, picked it up and returned to my bed. I sat down heavily and surveyed the meagre offerings. The porridge was thin and watery and really not very palatable as usual and the Tealog was nothing like that which I was able to get, even on my ship. I sighed and slouched onto the bed. Another day closer to death.

I was just finishing the rubbish, sloppy porridge when I heard an alarm in the corridor. I had no idea why it was going off, such things were commonplace on large ships so I gave it little thought. After a few more seconds, the alarm changed in tone and became louder and more insistent. As I sat on the bed, I watched a small blue bolt of lightning jump from the end of the bed to the ground and back again. Then, a much larger bolt then zoomed across the room and left a scorch mark on the opposing wall. I hit the ground as yet another one shot out through the ceiling. I yelled as one more shot past my ear. The next spark was far larger and smashed into the control panel to the left of the doorway. Assorted other more normal looking sparks coruscated from the panel as the electrics fried. The door then made a sort of depressed "clunk" sound and popped open a few centimetres. I swigged the last of my revolting Tealog, sprang to my feet, ran across the room and wrenched the door as hard as I could. It didn't move so I kicked it repeatedly. It still didn't move. I stood back, tired from my exertions and rested my hands on my thighs and took a few deep breaths. A few seconds later another enormous spark shot from one side of the room to the other and smashed the door clean off its hinges. "Result!" I said and punched the air.

    I left the cell as quickly as I could. As I travelled down the dingy corridor, I could tell that the whole ship was in disarray. Guardians and assorted other people were scurrying around like headless chickens and no one paid any attention to me. Blue sparks zipped down the corridors from time to time and every so often there was a scream as they connected with some unfortunate soul. I followed the corridor back the way I'd been dragged a few days previously and found myself at a large crossroads. All the tunnels were identical and so I picked one at random. After a couple of minutes, this led to another corridor which ran parallel to the outside of the ship so I turned left. I'd not been along here before as it had windows and none of the corridors I'd seen up until then had any of these. This should have meant I would have been able to look out into the darkness beyond but much of the window I was passing was obscured by a pale gelatinous substance which stopped me from seeing out. The next window along was clear of this but I was able to see the gelatinous thing stretching off into the distance. I only looked out for a short while as every so often, blue sparks would travel down it and earth themselves across the corridor. These electrical discharges were playing havoc with the ship as I could hear little explosions as various subsystems on board failed and then exploded.

There was no need to run anywhere so I slowed down to a normal walking pace. I really didn't want to attract unnecessary attention. As I walked about in the chaos, it seemed the sparks were more powerful than when I had left the cell and they were more regular. It seemed wiser to stay close to the ground so I hunkered down. More sparks shot overhead and I realised that I could spot where they were starting. A tiny blue spot would appear on the outer hull before expanding and enlarging to a line. This would then zip across the hall forming an arc. As a waddled along, I noticed a large one forming on my left, quite low down. In a flash, I threw myself to the ground and lay and watched as a swarm of them buzzed overhead. They did seemed to have a pattern to them. There were about ten seconds between each pulse of electricity and, once I'd noted this, I could time my journey down the passageway. If I ran for eight seconds and then hit the deck as the sparks travelled from one end of the space to the other, as long as the sparks remained at the same time interval, I would be ok. I took several deep breaths, jumped to my feet and sprinted, throwing myself at the ground just before a large spark whizzed over my head. I felt the hair on the back of my skull burn as I got too close to it.

My journey consisted of a series punctuated sprints and spectacular dives. At the end, the corridor took a left. On the wall as I propelled myself towards the floor once more, I noted a map which indicated where I was. I was luckily on the right level of the ship to be able to get back to *The Cowrie* and make my escape however I was headed in the wrong direction. Shit. I looked down the passage and watched as a group of terrified looking people ran towards me.

"Get down!" I bellowed as loudly as I could, lying on the ground as I saw the spark heading up the corridor towards them.

One or two of them managed to get low enough to avoid being struck but the reminder did not react quickly enough and received lethal bolts of electricity, screamed horribly and fell to the ground. I waited until a spark passed over my head and sprinted off back the way I had come. Another few dives and I was back to the crossroads. I should have gone straight on rather than left. I barrelled on down the passageway as fast as I could, sporadically throwing myself to the ground. My knees and elbows were somewhat battered by now but I was getting closer to the landing bay. On the wall, there was another map which showed me that I was headed in the right direction, this time. A right turn, then second left and then another right and I should be there. I set off again, panting with the continued exertion. I was getting closer to my target. I'd seen fewer and fewer people on the last leg of my journey back to the landing bay. I surmised some must have managed to get into escape pods and had evacuated or died under the electrical onslaught. Certainly the screams were less frequent than they'd been when I had first escaped from my cell.

I rounded the last corner and dived through the already open doors to the landing bay. It was a honking great room and here the sparks seemed less inclined to jump from one end to the other, perhaps the size of the space was too large for them to arc. *The Cowrie* was in a corner, looking beaten up after the battle. However, she still looked spaceworthy and would do as an escape pod. The Union had not tried to break into the ship while I had been in the cell, they'd just left her parked up in the corner of the bay, presumably for later study after I was dead. I touched the palm print control panel and the ramp opened. Just then, a spark leapt across the room and earthed itself through the deck and the ramp, throwing me clear. I flew inelegantly through the air and landed a couple of metres away. I was slightly burnt, badly bruised and shaken but ok. I lay on the floor breathing heavily until I felt well enough to stand up. The sparks were certainly growing in intensity in here now as they regularly flashed from side to side in the room. They were also jumping from floor to ceiling and leaving large scorch marks as they did so. Hopefully once I was inside the ship I would be safe as it should act as a Faraday Cage and isolate me from any electrostatic discharges. This time, I sprinted up the ramp rather than dawdling and closed it up just as a spark formed. I threw myself inside the ship and closed up the ramp.

Once inside my ship, mentally I felt much better. I staggered to the back of the ship, grabbed a first aid kit and gave myself an injection of painkillers because everything hurt. Almost immediately I began to feel more human. I grabbed a spacesuit, put it on and walked quickly up to cockpit area, finally collapsing into the pilot's chair. I hurriedly sealed off the cockpit from the rest of the ship, in case there were any atmospheric leaks. Then I powered up the sensors and scanned the region. A few red lights lit up on the console but I ignored them. There were still four life signs on The Union ship but everyone else had gone. They were right over the other side of the craft and so I had no way to rescue them, besides which, they might well be rather hostile toward me. From the readings I obtained, I was also able to determine what was going on. The ship had clearly strayed too close to one of the giant jellyfish creatures in the Bok globule and was slowly being drawn up towards the mouthparts underneath the bell. The electrical discharges were probably to stun the prey, in this case the ship, before consuming it. I assumed that *The Cowrie* had been too small to bother with otherwise I might have found myself in a similar situation on the several occasions that I'd passed through this region of space. As I peered at the scanner, a massive bolt of lightning took out the bay doors and the whole bay depressurised. With the change in pressure, the ship began to slide inexorably towards the open doors. Thinking quickly, I fired up the manoeuvring thrusters, adjusted my course and headed for the open hatch. The ship pitched and wobbled with the gale which was quickly sucking the remaining atmosphere from the vast room and then we popped out into clear space like a rather large champagne cork emerging from a shaken bottle. The ship spun upside down, then righted itself with the help of the side jets and then, finally, some equilibrium returned. I tried to start the main engines but they refused to ignite so, using the thrusters, I flew away as quickly as I could from the creature and the stricken ship. Once at a safe distance, I stopped and remained in a stationary position and watched what was happening. Over the next few minutes the ship slowly imploded as the creature tightened its grip. The sparks became more and more powerful and then suddenly, the ship exploded. The energy from the explosion lit up the creature like a giant light bulb in space and it glowed orange as it absorbed the energy from the explosion. It then continued on its way, presumably looking for the next meal. It had been fascinating to watch – the jellyfish clearly fed on energy and used the electrical pulses to cause the prey to explode and release the energy that it fed on. The animal was presumably sated now so even at this small distance, I was safe.

    Once it had floated off a sufficiently large distance, I ran a diagnostic. I was immensely relieved to discover that, despite all the battering she'd taken, the ship was still air-tight. Only then, did I rest for a while with a nice cup of Tealog, checked on the FPO, which was really pleased to see me and then surveyed the damage to the ship in greater detail. Much of it was indeed superficial but some of the relays were burnt out, including the one which controlled the power supply to the main engines. These could easily be replaced from the inside and wouldn't take that long. More worrying was the damage to the outer hull. One of the direct hits from the lasers had come within millimetres of punching a hole all the way through the skin of the ship. This would require me to do a spacewalk and patch weld over the top. There also appeared to be a small leak from one of the electrical storage solution tanks which would require investigation. Again, this would also need patching. I'm not very keen on spacewalks, I find the whole experience dizzying and it tends to make me throw up but it was the only way to insure that I would be able to get back to Earth in one piece.

The Ventos Conspiracy 2

    I changed awkwardly into the spacesuit. It was uncomfortable and restrictive but it was all I had. I'd not expected to be doing this at all so I was glad I only had a couple of patches to do. I expected I would be outside for about an hour in total. I depressurised the airlock and stepped out into the darkness carrying a hold-all with my repair equipment. Looking around and fighting the urge to be sick, I could just see the jellyfish in the far distance, it looked tiny but was still glowing orange so it stood out like a beacon in the blackness. I switched on my magnetised boots and clumped around the ship to the first damaged area. The hole was not massive, it measured about ten centimetres across but it was clearly potentially very dangerous had I left it unchecked. Firstly, I filled the hole with the gloopy magnetic liquid filler and applied the patch over the top. The filler would cure on its own, even in the vacuum of space but the patch would need to be welded on over the top to get a tight seal. I fired up the space welder and carefully traced the outside edge of the patch. Under the infrasonic pulses, it fizzed and melted into the main skin of the ship and in a few minutes, the hole was safely patched.

    As I was outside, I scanned the outer hull in more detail in case the ship's sensors had missed anything. There was indeed a small leak in the electrical solution storage tank. As the space welder did not utilise hot material and relied on a flow of positively charged ions to repair the damage, there was no danger of fire. This hole required a similar, but smaller patch than the one I had just fitted but the damage was on the edge of the tank so the shape of it made it more difficult and it took a lot longer than I had anticipated. Luckily, the spacesuit had plenty of air reserves so after a total of an hour and a half of fighting back the nausea, I safely re-entered the ship. Safely inside, I ran a few preliminary checks, noted the lower number of red lights, had another cup of Tealog and set course for the other edge of the globule and Earth using only the thrusters. All the external repairs were completed and so once I was on my way, I could make running repairs to the remaining damaged systems internally. At least I was free from The Union and no one would have expected me to have survived the attack by the jellyfish creature. I did not feel the need to engage the camo drive, there wouldn't be anyone around and besides which, I needed to save the power for when I entered the Earth's orbit and atmosphere when I was more likely to be spotted by The Union.

    I spent the next week flying slowly through featureless space once more. Once or twice I spotted the jellyfish things but they were very far away and not a threat. Firstly, I replaced the broken relays for the main engines while the ship flew on autopilot. I then slowly replaced the others once again, I was back to flying at full speed. The FPO was happy to see me, it had not suffered while being left on its own as it just stayed deeply hidden in the dirt box, resurfacing when the automatic UV lamp had come on.

Within a couple of days, most systems were fully operational and, although power reserves were a little low, these could be topped up by a fly past the sun in our own solar system. I avoided the dead Earth system but the sensors did pick up some odd readings from the sun which was still sporadically throwing off shells of material, perhaps it was now back on the main sequence and might end its life the way it was supposed to, as a white dwarf – albeit several billion years too early. Humankind had clearly tried its level best to ruin things and, in this weird relict timeline, it had managed to wipe itself out.

I turned my attention to what to do next. I could do with an ally to help me to figure out a way to defeat The Union for once and for all. All of my old work contacts would be useless and anyone connected with the journalists that I used to know would be just as ineffective. I tried to think, I needed someone clever and independent who could see the connections between what was going on and the real life applications of it. They'd also have to be astute enough to understand the fragmented piece of space that I was currently flying through. The solution was actually quite obvious, I needed to talk to my old friend Professor Karl McDoughale. He was probably the only person smart enough to understand what was happening. Also, being an academic, he would be above suspicion by The Union who left the Universities to get on with their own business. They only really took interest in people who were under the age of thirty and able to work in the mines or those who were clearly young and geniuses. I needed to be near to Cambridge so that I could find him and explain the situation - there was an abandoned parking zone just outside the city at the Gog Magog Park. It had once been an area for local walkers to ramble around but with the expansion of the city, it had gradually been developed into a massive car park. The single remaining green space, near Wandlebury Hill was a large field and so would be a good place to stop. It was nicely accessible but little used these days so no one would be expecting anyone to be there. With the decrease in the population following the third virus outbreak, the city, along with many others had contracted so around the periphery were buildings that were largely abandoned. From the landing spot, it was an easy few kilometres walk to the centre of the city where the colleges were.

    The last of the internal repairs were fully completed just as I reached the edge of the globule. It had been a dull journey and I was relieved to feel the slight drag as the ship popped back into normal space. I immediately activated the camo drive and checked that the course was correctly set for Earth. I had programmed it so I would fly in from behind the Sun, charge up the solar cells and also be shielded from anyone who might be watching. That was still another couple of weeks away though so I busied myself with exercises, getting even better prepared for my stint back on Earth.

Chapter three – Cambridge

I landed on a dry and bright morning in July. It was warm but not unreasonably so. There had not been any problems on the remainder of my journey back to Earth. The ship was now fully charged so I could leave the camo drive running for weeks. I packed up my essentials in a backpack, plus a few pieces of technology which could prove useful, put the FPO carefully into my pocket and set off. There was nobody around as I trudged along the main road. Every so often, I stopped for a drink and around 1pm, lunch, which I took in a nice large field which had presumably once been cultivated. It now contained lots of small, sturdy trees and large expanses of tall, unkempt hassocks of grass. My only company, aside from the FPO were a few rabbits running about and the odd blackbird. Aside from that, I saw no one. It was only about five kilometres from where I had left the ship to the centre of Cambridge and so the walk was not a long one and it was rather pleasant with the sun shining and a light breeze blowing across the former fields. As I got closer to the city, I noticed changes in the landscape and signs of former human activity became more obvious. The large buildings on the outer edges of the city were all but derelict; many businesses had folded once the population had shrunk and no one had been around to occupy them or patronise them. The whole effect was rather spooky especially with a few animals which were moving about inside them causing me to jump a few times as I passed by. The road was not in the best of repair either, The Union only really took care of areas it deemed important and the road leading from Suffolk to Cambridgeshire clearly wasn't a priority.

I walked past the old abandoned Addenbrooke's Hospital on the way and, after an hour and a half of pleasant ambling, I reached the middle of the city. The spires of the old colleges were still there and the skyline hadn't changed since my last visit. The Union considered Cambridge to be an out of the way part in the East of the country and so hadn't bothered to repair the infrastructure and didn't really encourage people to go there. Anyone who was here was purely to make sure architecturally interesting buildings were occupied, maintained and to provide security or be one of a few dozen students who occupied the dorms in the university. There were a couple of lecturers besides the professor but I barely knew them and I was fairly sure that they wouldn't be able to help me even if they wanted to.

I reached the main doors in the small pedestrianised section of the city. They were massive wooden dread portals, studded with metal and a small window on the left hand side. Not far away were the derelict remains of an abandoned factory which looked as though it would fall down at any minute and all around were large signs saying "Keep Out" "Private" and so on. I took a deep breath and knocked on the door.

    A small, scruffy sunburnt face appeared at the Judas door, partly obscured by a flat black hat.
"Wot do you want?" it asked imperiously.
"I'd like to speak to Professor Karl McDoughale?" I asked cautiously.
"Why?" was the response.
"I should have said, I'm an old friend of his and I happened to be passing."
"He's not accepting visitors at the moment." said the porter and slammed the little door.
I knocked again harder and it slid open with a distinct air of hostility.
"I told you..." he said.
"I know," I said cutting him off mid-sentence, "but can you tell him it's urgent, please – it concerns The McDoughale Effect and its effects on space / time."
"Wot?" he replied.
"It's all rather complicated to explain, I just need to talk to him, please? I'm not going anywhere until you let me in."
"Right," he said thoughtfully scratching his stubbly chin, "ok then, I'll let you in if you can you tell me what the name of his daughter's dog is?"
    This was clearly a trick question as she didn't own a dog, however, she did have a psychotic feline that I had met a few times so I smiled and said:

"She doesn't have a dog, it's a cat and it's called Willikins" I retorted.

After a few seconds he paused, gurned slightly and replied:

"Yes, that's right." With that, he sighed, pulled another face and finally opened the door.

I walked into a large open courtyard bounded on three sides by cloisters, in the centre was a green space with an immaculate lawn. I was led along the passageway to a steep flight of stairs which disappeared up into the darkness. My guide pointed upwards and said:

"Up there, through the door, along the corridor about five metres, second door on the right – you can't miss it, it says Lucasian Professor of Mathematics"

"OK, thanks." I said and trotted up the stairs.

Once within the confines of the building, the architecture was more like something you'd see in a gothic temple but surprisingly it wasn't too hard to find the right door. I knocked gently and waited.

"Yes?" came a melodious voice from the other side.

"Professor McDoughale?" I asked

"Yes?" came the more confident reply.

"May I come in please? It's Paul Heath. I have something very important I have to talk to you about."

There was a long pause and then the door opened. In front of me stood the professor – not looking much different to when I'd last seen him a few years earlier. He was of medium height, probably about sixty, slim with a shock of manic black hair atop his head. He wore small round rimmed glasses and an air of bright intelligence while at the same time managing to seem friendly and approachable. Knowing him quite well, I would categorise him as "frighteningly intelligent". In my life, I'd only met three other people who fell into that category and two of them had been my bosses at work. They were the sort of people who you could have had a discussion about fractals with one minute and then renaissance painting the next. They seemed to know everything about everything. When I had first met him, some years before, he had been extremely kind and considerate however, I had heard several years back that his wife had died and he was now estranged from his daughter and her family. Press reports had said he'd taken to drinking too much red wine and now devoted all his spare time to working. He'd become ostracised from his colleagues, almost given up teaching and become a bit of a recluse. He had also become increasingly vocal in his opposition to The Union and its way of doing things. However, despite my description of him as my friend and his often patronising manner, I was always slightly in awe of him due to his astounding intellect.

"Ah, Paul." he said in a fairly friendly fashion, shook my hand firmly and said "Haven't seen you for ages. How's the ex?"

I thought for a second and responded that I'd not seen her in years and that I didn't know where she was.

"Pity," he replied somewhat lasciviously, "such a charming young woman!" and grinned at me.

I shook my head and said:

"Not by the end. It was all a long time ago now and I don't think of her much these days. Time is a funny thing, sometimes it seems like it was only yesterday that we were together and yet, at other times, it seems like an eternity."

"Ah," he replied with a twinkle in his eye, "just remember that the last ten years are merely a lot of yesterdays stacked one after the other."

"Good point." I replied and smiled. He beckoned me through the open door and said
"Come in and tell me what ails thee."

I nodded and waited while he paused briefly before making his way quickly back to a plush armchair to the left of an enormous old fireplace and motioned that I should move a pile of paper from it. I placed that carefully in the only free space on the floor. Although there was no fire burning in the fireplace, the room was comfortably warm. Once sitting down, I looked around – the rest of the place looked like a bomb had hit it. Papers were strewn everywhere, the bookshelves were in complete disarray and there were scribbled notes all around, pinned onto the wainscoting, stuck to the bare walls and a very old fashioned whiteboard which was covered in horribly complex looking mathematical equations. In the corner there was an ancient long case clock which ticked away to itself. Even this had notes stuck to the front of it. I remembered that he was very old fashioned in some ways, hence the clock and the white board. These days, most people used invisiboards and rewritable paper but he clearly didn't have any truck with those, at least here in his inner sanctum. He made himself comfortable on a worn looking luxurious leather sofa and then he leaned back, steepled his fingers, peered at me over the top of his circular spectacles:

"So then, my old chum, what's all this about then?"

I paused briefly and then recounted the whole story, from my break up with my fiancée all the way through to my space battle with The Union ships. I commented especially on the relict section of the timeline within the Bok globule I'd found and what I had discovered on the dead Earth. He listened, fingers still steepled in front of his face, eyes half closed - clearly relishing the details that I included and periodically asking questions when he wanted clarification. It took a good couple of hours to explain the situation to him and by then, the evening was drawing in. I also showed him the FPO which he appeared rather disinterested in, probably because it was biological and not a maths or physics problem that could be solved. After I stopped talking, he leaned forward and breathed deeply. He rang a small bell and a porter arrived with a nice large glass of Rioja for us both.

"Right" he said cheerfully, "I do have a few thoughts. It's totally obvious that The Union is up to something, I've long suspected that things are not quite as good as they seem and they are far more of a threat than we all imagine. I've tried to promulgate this idea however, even among the academic staff, few are willing to listen to me or take any kind of stand against them. I do often wonder if I could do a better job than that bunch of Johnsons!" he concluded with a hint of irony.

He took a sip of wine and continued:

"That ore you've spoken about sounds rather interesting. I'd love to get the geological department to have a look at it! It would also be scientifically valid to see if exposure to it has any long term physiological effects on those who come in contact with it," he eyed me closely and the continued:

"You seem very attached to your little animal. Interesting that it has a well-developed defence system that seems to respond to anger and you yourself said you were feeling different."

He paused for a second:

"Leading on from that, I have to say that you do seem, how should I put this...different to when I last saw you. You're much more confident, you look like you've spent ages in a gym and there is an angriness behind your eyes which I don't recall ever having seen before. I do wonder if the ore has altered your personality in some way. I suppose it might be down to you having spent so long on your own or might also be that you're shit-scared as The Union is obviously after you. Whatever it is, you've obviously become far more aggressive and much more up for a fight."

He paused for breath. I said nothing for a minute.

"Yes." I responded slowly, "I certainly feel different but in a good way."

He finally stood up but remained silent for a minute, taking another mouthful of wine and looking out of the large windows across the quad.

"All that said, that's quite a tale," he said turning round slowly.

"I assume you need my help?"

I nodded enthusiastically.

"Ok but I suggest you get some rest. You'll be safe here and there is an empty room just down the hallway. I'll let the porter know that you are staying to help me with some research. We'll need to go to my lab tomorrow as I simply must take a look at the Bok globule again in case your actions have made any changes which might lead to a new discovery and another paper! When you're settled into your room, ring for a porter and he'll bring you some supper. There's a bell beside the fireplace. Tell him it's important that no one knows you are here. Now, I absolutely must continue with my work."

      I left after I'd finished my wine. The room was a few metres away down the corridor. It was spacious and had clearly once been an office but with so few people around, it was now used as a guest apartment. The bed was freshly made and the towels were clean. I dumped the backpack on the bed and let the FPO out to stretch its prongs. It had remained quiet and still during my chat with the professor and clearly welcomed the chance to run about a bit. It seemed pleased to be back on a planet and, despite the gravity being stronger than Ventos, it was adjusting quickly. I was tired and could certainly do with some food. I did as I had been instructed and soon a large quantity of very good food was brought to me in the room a short while later fortunately by a different porter to the miserable one I had spoken to at the door.

      I slept soundly that night. The building creaked and groaned due to its age but this did not prevent my dropping off immediately and sleeping like a log for eight solid hours – something which I very rarely do. I awoke refreshed and ready for whatever was going to happen next. I sat around for a while happily digesting a nice cooked breakfast and then around 9.30am I put the FPO into an empty fish tank filled with soil (which the porter had reluctantly provided) and left it to itself to sleep. Afterwards, I walked down the corridor and tentatively knocked on the professor's door. He answered it and greeted me affably. For his age, he was remarkably sprightly and fresh looking - this was even more of a surprise to me when he said he said he'd been up since 05:30 working on a new paper on the theoretical physics of wormholes.

"Right", he said in that peculiarly English way which people do before embarking on something of import, "Let's go!"

He led me down the stairs to the square, out through the door and into the street. Just opposite was a sunken parking area. Humankind had not yet given up its addiction to cars and many of them had been stored underground and not used while the pandemics raged. Due to the reduction in the population and the far fewer drivers around, vehicular congestion and pollution had all but disappeared. They did not run on petrol or batteries but had all been converted to run on hydrogen. There were so many safety protocols in place using that system that explosions were a virtual impossibility and no one had died in a hydrogen explosion since the previous century.

The professor retrieved a small remote control unit from his jacket pocket and pressed a button in the middle. A sleek, elegant looking car ascended from the parking area on a plinth and then started up and drove slowly towards us. It stopped a metre away and the doors opened silently.

"Wow!" I said, "Nice car!"

"Thanks," he replied, "you might note that I have made a few modifications to it too." He grinned again.

We climbed in. He pressed a few buttons on the dashboard and the car began to move slowly, edging towards the paved road. It then accelerated rapidly to a steady cruising speed of sixty five kilometres an hour. The professor touched a couple of buttons and settled back in his seat while the car drove itself. Like all cars, the professor's vehicle was controlled by inlaid instructions in the road surface via a system called AIRS – Artificially Intelligent Road System. The car's AI control system interfaced directly with AIRS and adjusted itself to the current traffic conditions so accidents never happened. Any emissions were kept to a minimum and also that no one was ever prosecuted for speeding because there wasn't technically a limit.

"We'll be there in an hour or so," he said. "You might as well make yourself comfortable."

We drove off out of the city and out towards the motorway. As there was no other traffic, the car effortlessly accelerated to one hundred and eighty kilometres an hour and sped along the fairly well maintained roadway. Any bumps and lumps were absorbed by the adaptive suspension which changed depending on the pitch of the road noise. We joined the top deck of the M25 and headed off around it. As expected, there was little traffic and so our speed remained constant. We turned off at one of the junctions near Guildford and sped along the main road, at a slower speed than on the motorways. Soon, we were in deepest Surrey and pretty little villages were flashing past as we drove along. Eventually, the roads narrowed and we turned down a side road. Here the tyres auto-inflated to adapt to the different terrain and we drove down a dirt track for maybe three kilometres. On the left hand side was a roadway which seemed surprisingly intact and we drove along for another kilometre before it widened out to a large carpark. The professor selected a parking space, let the car park itself and we got out. He retrieved a knapsack from the boot and slung it over his left shoulder.

"This way," he said cheerily, pointing up to the entrance. "We do have to do this bit on foot, I'm afraid," he added grinning apologetically. We walked up the driveway towards the imposing entrance, a stunning edifice of glass and polycrete. He held his pass up to the doorway and it beeped and allowed us to enter. We walked in, with the professor leading the way.

The entrance hall was cavernous and bright with all the light that entered through the enormous expanses of clear bioplastic window. There were two (I thought) overly ornate staircases on the left and right hand side of the entrance, directly ahead. Situated between those was another door.

"Through here," he said softly.

The room was a tiny square area, like an airlock and, on the opposing wall to the right of a large fire door was a flat metal plate at roughly head height. The professor walked right up to it, stopped about three centimetres away and stuck out his tongue so it was in contact with the plate. The wall shuddered and a large door opened up as a little electronic voice said, "Identity confirmed, access accepted."

I looked on, bewildered by what had just happened.

"Ah," said the professor knowingly, "it's done on a microscopic analysis of the papillae on my tongue. If anyone who the system doesn't recognise tries it, the security system can also deliver a lethal electric shock! Clever eh?"

"But what about me?" I asked slowly.

"You're ok, I can let you in once I am properly inside," he replied and disappeared into the room beyond.

"Ok then, I'll see you in a minute," I said unnecessarily.

I stood alone in the tiny room and hummed a short phrase of Schubert to myself and about thirty seconds later, the door opened again and the professor ushered me into the main lab.

The Ventos Conspiracy 2

	We strode into a space about twenty metres square. The professor then busied himself flicking some switches on the wall and causing the lights to come on. Once these had reached full brightness, I could see that the lab was stuffed full of equipment, much of it unfamiliar to me. The professor didn't stay still for long, he flitted across the lab muttering to himself as he flicked switches and turned dials and generally looked busy. Gradually, gigantic computers lit up, things whirred and overhead, a gigantic circular portal slid noiselessly open.
	"Very impressive!" I said.
	"Thanks," he replied, just as an enormous telescope slid out of the side of the lab and angled itself to point through the roof.
	"It doesn't matter that it's daylight," he explained, "the optics are adaptive and can compensate for that. The 'scope here is also connected to the observing station on the far side of the moon and so we can create an enormous apparent aperture width with no distortion due to the distance. The aperture is in the order of three hundred and eighty five thousand kilometres and using this, we can see further than any other telescope ever constructed by humans to date. It's this which enabled me to see the image of the Bok globule in remarkably fine detail and the readings I obtained meant I could theorise the physics to be able to see through it."
	"Clever stuff!" I said in awe.

He walked over to a large display screen and peered at it thoughtfully. He picked at his lip with his index finger and frowned.

"What's up?" I asked.

"The readings are all off. Something's gone awry. The globule is dissipating and becoming transparent. See, look for yourself."

I walked over to him and looked at the screen. Instead of the massive black expanse that I had observed close to, there was a sort of milky looking opacity to the whole region. Every so often, bright spots would emerge in random locations and then fade away after a second or two. It was like observing a glass of milk with flakes of glitter surfacing in it.

"That's really weird." I said.

"Yes. Never seen anything like that before, I'll leave the equipment running and see if I can determine anything from a bigger data set."

He pulled up a chair and sat down. "I'll be a few minutes," he said offhandedly, "just amuse yourself but please don't touch anything."

I stood there for a few seconds, feeling excluded and trying to figure out how to do this. In the end, I scratched my head and grabbed the nearest chair and sat down. Not many people got to watch a genius at work, he'd not even had a Ph.D. student for over a decade so this was a real treat.

Unfortunately, as he sat there scribbling on an invispad which emerged from the desk, there actually wasn't much that I could do. So I decided to listen to some music files on my portable chronometer for a while. When I looked up, all I could see were strings of equations on the screen and every time these appeared, the number at the end appeared in a bright red colour and was dismissed with a hand gesture. Then the professor would make a grunting noise and continue with another line of impossibly complex symbols and numbers. The maths must have been horrendous but still he kept picking away at the problem. Time and again the text was dismissed and he restarted. He was getting increasingly annoyed as each successive permutation failed to generate a solution which was satisfactory. After half an hour, he was clearly quite irritated and glowering at the screen muttering almost constantly. Words like "numpty", "dipstick" "pillock" and "cretin" were regularly used as each string of writing disappeared. The longer he sat there the more profane and loud his exclamations became but eventually he stopped and stared boggle eyed at the screen.

"It's fucking gone!" he yelled at the top of his voice. "What the fuckity fuck is happening? That's totally fucking impossible. Shit! Bollocky, shitty, shit, fuck!!"

He spun round, his usually pale features were flushed red. He was shaking with anger, his fists clenched and clearly almost incoherent with rage. He then pointed furiously at the screen. Instead of the black blob or the white opaque region of space, there was a perfectly clear star field. Beyond it, visible in crystal clear space was the Ventos system in all its glory, the third planet shining like a white snooker ball. The nuclear winter had clearly not subsided at all and the whole planet was little more than a sold ball of ice. However, at this range, it was actually rather beautiful.

I stood for several minutes open mouthed looking at the screen while the professor's rage gradually subsided.

"I suppose you didn't expect that?" I asked questioningly after what seemed like an appropriate length of time.

He beamed at me, his rage all but dissipated.

"Nope, not at all. However, I do think I have enough data here to write another paper – even if that event happened a few weeks ago!"

"Oh, that's good," I said disinterestedly. "So what now?"

He paused for a minute, I could practically hear the cogs grinding in his head.

"Hmm...I'll just send the data to my office back in Cambridge and to the car and then we need to think about your other problem."

He clicked a few buttons and, in a surprisingly short period of time, turned around and said we could leave.

"But I wanted to know what all this stuff does?" I asked imploringly indicating some of the equipment in the lab.

"Another time, my impatient old chum – we have bigger fish to fry!"

"Ok then." I said despondently as the telescope retracted into its housing and the lights dimmed.

With that, the discussion was over and we retraced our steps from the lab, back out via the lethal doorway and to the main entrance. We paused briefly at the coffee machine which luckily also dispensed Tealog and after a sit down on the benches outside the building enjoying the sunshine, we returned to the car. Once settled in and back on the big roads, I asked him about the time issues with the newly acquired experimental data. He agreed it was a definite problem but no one else could possibly have seen what we had just seen due to the power of the telescope – due to its massive aperture, we could see further back in time than anyone else on the planet. After that, he lent me some credit chips, in case I needed them, and then we headed back to Cambridge.

He said little on the remainder of the drive back to Cambridge, appearing to be very deep in thought. He was still quiet even after a mid-afternoon drink which consisted of another very good bottle of red. After a couple of hours, I found that I was tired and slightly bored and so decided to return to my room, my music collection and the FPO which I thought would probably want to have a run about by now. The professor clearly could only spend a limited time in other people's company before he became bored so it was best to not be around him too much. Besides which, he'd have plenty of new data to go over and my problem with The Union still needed solving.

I walked into my room. It was a mess, someone had clearly been in while I was out. Surely the porters would only let people in under strict instructions? I had also taken care to lock the door on the way out and it clearly hadn't been forced. The next thing I noticed was the dirt filled fish tank was on its side, the dirt was all over the floor and there was no sign of the FPO. I then proceeded to turn the room upside down even more looking for my little green friend. I even tried making friendly sounding squeaking noises to attract it but it was clearly nowhere to be found. It was abundantly clear that someone had broken in and kidnapped it. Nothing else seemed to be missing but whoever it was had clearly been looking for something as well as the FPO. I shook my head in anger and disbelief – who would do that? Before the thought had barely left my consciousness, I was obvious to me that The Union had to be involved. That meant they knew I was here which also meant that one of the ships must have got a signal off before it had been destroyed in the Bok globule. I really had no idea what to do. Speaking to the professor was a bad idea, he'd just be grumpy and he'd been fairly disinterested in my little companion anyway. I sat on the bed and put my head in my hands and tried to think. However, I soon realised that sitting there thinking really didn't make any difference so I decided to go for a walk. Before I did so, I set up a perimeter alarm on the door, linked to my belt so that I would get a warning and a visual record if someone entered my room while I was out.

I left via the main entrance, looking left and right in case I was being observed. There was no one about that I could see. There also didn't appear to be any sort of electronic surveillance devices nearby. Anyway, it was a pleasant early evening with a light breeze blowing a few leaves around. There were few people milling about so I just walked around the centre of the city looking at the ancient architecture and generally passing the time. Those who were around appeared to be tourists and a few harassed looking people who looked as though they had somewhere to be. Although the pace of life had slowed as there were less humans around, there were still a few die-hard workaholics (including the professor) who felt it necessary to run about as if their tasks were the most important things in the entire world. I didn't subscribe to that theory and I had always done enough at work but not bothered to go the extra distance. At least if you are average at work, they didn't earmark you for greater things and my work ethic gave me time to concentrate on the really important things in life.

I remembered Cambridge briefly from my previous visits and, at least on the face of it, it hadn't changed a great deal – not that I expected it to have done so. The construction industry was all but dead as there were literally millions of surplus homes after the final pandemic – effectively making homelessness a thing of the past. The whole retail sector had moved almost entirely to The Network. Payments were usually made by retinal scans from home and everyone had a scanner hooked up to their computers. Compared to pre-pandemics, there was actually not a great deal going on with the human race. People still made discoveries (like the professor) but The Union had cornered the work market and everyone had to do their stint mining either on the Moon or, like I had done, out in the asteroid belt. However, even at this time, that was beginning to be depleted of useful materials and they had begun to look elsewhere. Presumably, the end point of that search for energy and resources would be the destruction of the planet after the sun was harvested. I absolutely had to stop this.

I wandered down Jesus Lane. According to the plaque at one end, there had once been a whole series of restaurants and bars along there, these had all but gone but there was still one left that was open so I decided to stop off for a drink, a meal and try to think. The building was clearly repurposed from some sort of old fashioned town house, it had ornate ceilings and some interesting wood panelling and a very old long case clock ticking unobtrusively in the far corner. The establishment was surprisingly busy. There were a few young couples sat at the nice wooden tables and the odd older patrons were discussing how badly behaved the younger generation were and, of course, the weather. The atmosphere was generally one of convivial cheerfulness. There was a large 3D hologrammatic screen in the corner of the room which was showing whatever nonsense passed for TV these days. I looked at my chronometer as I selected one of the empty tables and sat down. It was almost 7pm. I ordered Tealog and a hamwich in the usual fashion, using the keypad which was set into the table. Within a minute of paying using the credit chips the professor had lent me earlier, a small robot trundled over with my order, slid it onto the table and printed out a receipt. It turned away and buzzed off back to the robot storage area to the left of the bar. Just then, an attention grabbing noise indicated that a news bulletin was on. It was full of the usual rubbish, all depressing nonsense controlled by The Union and mostly consisted of pointless drivel about meaningless micro celebrities. As if to serve as a reminder that they were in control, the top right hand side of the display proudly displayed The Union logo which from time to time would rotate, explode into a billion tiny pieces which scattered across the screen and then reform. I glanced at it and let the tedium wash over me. I never really had much interest in the news so paid it little attention. Although the sound was down it was easy to follow the stories as they were broadcast just by glancing at it periodically. I've often wondered why when there is a screen in the room, humans feel a compulsive urge to look at it, even if they are not bothered about what is on. Maybe that was something the professor could answer?

After finishing my hamwich, I was just taking a sip of my tea when my photo appeared on the screen – sure, it was me as I had been before I'd got rid of my beard and had a decent haircut but it was definitely me. There was a caption at the bottom of the screen saying wanted for inciting insurrection. Someone in the bar laughed at the screen and flicked the screen off commenting that "It was a load of old bollocks" and this met with general amusement and agreement from the other patrons. I watched in horror as another figure stood up and said, very forthrightly, that he'd "rather listen to someone being sick in metal bucket for half an hour solid than hear any more propaganda from The Union". He looked vaguely familiar and while I sat there cowering in my chair, it dawned on me that it was one of my former mining colleagues. Granted, I was a few years older and somewhat different in appearance to when we'd last met but I was filled with a sense of dread that he might still be able to recognise me. My brain worked frantically, trying to think of a solution. However, as I watched hunkered lower down at my table, he swigged the last of his Tealog, shook his head determinedly and strolled out purposefully without giving anyone else in the place a second look.

Although I hated to admit it, I was somewhat rattled by the close call with a former colleague and, more importantly, the news. Admittedly, I was rather different in my appearance now to how I had been in the photograph but someone with half a brain could easily figure out from that I was the man from the image on the screen. Even if that didn't happen, if The Union started to issue photos of how I could hypothetically look without a beard and a lot less hair, then I would be easily identifiable. As my concerns filled my mind, I grew increasingly worried, about myself and the FPO so I swiftly finished my drink and left. I also wondered why they'd taken it – was it to lure me into a trap or was something else more sinister going on? Out in the lane again, I headed straight for the college. I would have to remain within its confines where I was likely to be safe from prying eyes until I made my move. I now needed a plan to rescue the FPO which meant that I would need to find out where it was being held. The chances are that an important discovery such as that would be taken to the main British centre of operations either near Derby or possibly the worldwide HQ in Poland. This would be complicated by my photo being plastered all over the news, making travel far more difficult.

As I turned left out of Jesus Lane, I spotted a man in a distinctive blue suit who was clearly a Guardian. He was on his own and not really paying attention to anything much at all. He just seemed to be enjoying the pleasantly warm evening like many others who stood around. My heart rate increased as I strolled by, as nonchalantly as possible on the other side of the road. Luckily, he seemed too busy standing around to pay any attention to a random passer-by.

There were a few other people around now, mostly students and tourists, just passing the time of day. As I got closer to the college I noticed it was growing increasingly dark. A cold light breeze sprang up and there was distant rumbling in the distance. Looking at my personal chronometer, it informed me that a level eleven storm was on the way. It was obvious from the clouds which were piling up in the sky that for once, the weather reports were correct and we were in for a storm. I love thunderstorms, there is something elemental about the whole spectacle and, as a result of the damage done to the climate in earlier centuries, now they are more powerful, frequent and unpredictable in nature than they had been. Presumably in the distant future when the damage was properly reversed, the climate would settle into some sort of natural equilibrium as it had been before humans had messed about with it. However, until then, we had to deal with squally and energetic storms and quite powerful tornadoes from time to time. These were especially frequent in summer and, after all, it had been a nice day so the heat would have built up sufficiently to trigger one of these storms. It was clearly developing quickly as, by the time I approached the doorway, enormous drops of rain began to fall. I hammered on the door and the porter let me in. We exchanged pleasantries, I made a quip about staying indoors with a cup of Tealog and he retorted that he couldn't as he was on duty. I responded with the fact that he'd need a brolly which he smirked at and concurred with. We parted on reasonable terms.

As I ascended the stairs back to my room, the heavens opened. It was going to be a terrific storm. Once back in my room, I sat on the bed in my chamber looking out as lightning flashed across the quad, throwing ancient buttresses into sharp relief. The rain was torrential and within a few minutes, the whole central area was a soggy mass of wet grass. The wind blew the droplets and hail around and they smacked hard into the windows making the panels rattle. Lightning split the sky and thunder made the ground shake. I sat there and contemplated the maelstrom outside. At least it wasn't a full on snowstorm like on Ventos and I wasn't out in it.

I watched for perhaps half an hour while the storm continued and then in a slight lull, I noticed a funnel cloud forming in the distance, over the roof of the college. These weren't uncommon now but this one had a particularly menacing look to it and it seemed as though it might possibly make contact with the ground. As I watched it, it snaked elegantly downwards and quickly formed a stable pillar of rotating debris. By this stage, it was very close and as I watched it progress towards the college, the noise became incredibly loud. The central pillar passed within ten metres of my window so I was able to get a good view as it blasted by, leaving a trail of devastation behind it. As suddenly as it had begun, it coiled itself back up into the cloud and was gone. A short while later, the rain stopped and the sun came out again. Everything was drenched and tree branches and other debris were liberally scattered about on the formerly tidy lawn. I made myself some more Tealog and put some music on. There was no point in going out again today so I made myself comfortable and eventually, it occurred to me that the only thing I could do was to wait for the professor to come up with a plan. I then dozed off.

I awoke hours later in total darkness. There was shouting and yelling from somewhere and someone was hammering on my door. I roused myself and walked over to it. The porter stood on the other side breathing heavily and looking very upset.

"It's the professor," he gasped, "he's been injured!"

I followed him quickly along the corridor to the professor's room. He opened the door. The professor was lying on the floor looking rather less dapper than usual. Blood was streaked on his face and torso and visible even through his shirt, he had a large and nasty looking open wound on his right arm. It was obvious what had happened; several of the large ancient window panes had blown in, showering him with fragments of glass. This must have happened during the tornado and he'd been in the way as the pane disintegrated and had been hit by the flying debris. I knelt down by his body and rolled up his sleeve to have a look at the wound. The first thing I noticed, just above the elbow was a metal bracelet. My stomach lurched. The professor had been under the influence of The Union all along! I quickly pulled the thing off his arm and threw it into the corner of the room. Remembering my first aid training, I tied a tourniquet around the top of his arm and carefully dressed the wound. I placed temposkin from a first aid kit which the porter had brought over the numerous smaller cuts and once this was done, between us we lifted him over to his bed. He was now awake but very groggy so the porter disappeared and returned with a cup of Tealog a few moments later. The professor smiled weakly at me.

"Thank you." was all he said before he slipped into unconsciousness.

He spent the next twenty four hours recuperating from the injuries he'd sustained. Although I was very on edge, the porter was extremely adept at getting whatever he asked for whether it was a boiled egg or a pizza. He was actually quite genial and enjoyed a chat. After delivering a rather splendid lunch, including a nice bottle of Rioja, he told me of the discovery of a body in the River Cam, not far from Fitzwilliam College. It was of "an unidentified thirty something year old male". It wasn't too much of a leap of imagination on my part to surmise that it might be the man from the tea bar. Presumably, someone must've overheard his comment and reported him to The Union. This did little to settle my mind so, in order to calm myself down, I headed out to the quad for some exercise. I ran through the entire military drills that I'd memorised while in the ice cavern and then did a few assorted push ups and sit ups on the lawn which, although still slightly muddy, was now mercifully free of debris from the tornado. This helped clear my mind for a while. Afterwards, I returned to the room, finished my wine and pondered what to do next. Despite the apparent danger, I risked a short evening walk to try to clear my head again but I took the evil bracelet with me too. I got as far as the River Cam where I launched it into the water. As far as I was concerned, it could stay there forever.

The Ventos Conspiracy 2

The following day, the professor seemed mostly himself; still a little weak but wanting to get back to work. Neither the porter nor I mentioned the elephant in the room, the mind control bracelet. Oddly, after the removal of the bracelet, there seemed little change to the professor's temperament from before the accident but he somehow seemed more peaceful and less driven than before – presumably the mind control device made him push himself harder than he would under normal circumstances. Hopefully the tantrum he'd thrown in the lab was also just a side effect of that too. By the next day, he was raring to go. I found him sitting at his terminal at 09:00 typing furiously away at some complex physics problem. He was back to his usual dapper self and grinned broadly at me as I entered.

"Morning old chap." he said chirpily.

"Morning, professor. How are you today?" I asked cautiously.

"Absolutely fine thanks," he responded cordially. "Just working on a little something that needs finishing, I'll be done in a minute."

Half an hour later, he was still furiously typing away and muttering quietly to himself although, interestingly, no expletives were involved. I noted that his cup of morning coffee had gone stone cold so he'd clearly been up for a while.

I gave up waiting and returned to my room and sat on the bed. After the drama of the tornado and the horrific weather of the night of the storm, the sunshine had reasserted itself and more normal summertime conditions had returned. It was another lovely summer's day so I sat and watched the small fluffy clouds float gently by on the breeze for a few minutes. I then grabbed a book from the collection and sat down on the bed and read. Who would have thought that Aardvarks were so interesting? After a few minutes, I opened the window and took several deep breaths of the pleasantly warm air and then I returned to my book. At 10:00 I again went through to see what the professor was up to. He was actually on his feet this time and was stretching his arms and jogging about in an effort to get himself moving after having sat still at his terminal, presumably for some time.

"Ah, Paul, there you are," he said cheerfully. "We need to discuss what's going on."

I nodded in agreement, sat down and reiterated my findings.

"Why did you want to go to your lab the other day?" I asked him carefully.

"I don't rightly know," he said slowly, "it just seemed like a compulsion that needed to be obeyed, must've been because of that damn bracelet thingy they made me wear."

"How long had you been wearing it?" I asked.

"Oh, I don't know, about a year, I think. My morning reports were supposed to have been filed with The Union at 6am every morning which is why I was getting up so early to work. By now they will have twigged that something is awry so we ought to make plans quickly."

I nodded in agreement.

"Where is it now?" he asked.

"At the bottom of the river," I replied.

"Great." he said forcefully. "I will not have people messing with my mind for any reasons whatsoever. That is simply not on. The only one who is allowed to mess with my mind is me and only with the use of alcohol! Free will is utterly and fundamentally important and to think you can subvert it like that is utterly despicable. They absolutely must be stopped!" as he spoke, he slammed his fist down on the desk at regular intervals. He was obviously furious and by the end of the sentence, he was almost shouting.

"Right," he paused for breath and then continued with slightly less vigour. "The upshot is you need to get your FPO back and we need to discredit The Union and expose their plan and put a stop to their meddling in worldwide affairs for once and for all."
Again I nodded and said:

"You'll get no disagreement from me."

"I thought not!" he said quickly at normal speaking volume and smiled.

He stood up, downed his now stone cold coffee, winced and wondered over to his monitor. It was still covered in calculations from the physics he'd been working on earlier. He wiped the screen clear with a swipe of his hand and sat down. I must've looked horrified as he said:

"It's ok" he said, sensing my concern, "it's all saved."

"Where now?" I asked.

"To the car, to your ship and then on to Derby!"

Chapter four – Midlands

We strolled out of the building, it hadn't taken either of us long to pack so it was still quite early in the day. We waved goodbye to the porter who just looked bored. Noticeably, he had a shredded umbrella propped up beside his little kiosk so he'd clearly tried to take my advice from a few days earlier, perhaps unwisely - either that or he was having a joke. As we turned out of the building, I noticed a Guardian milling about on the corner a few metres away. I wasn't sure but it looked like the one I had seen previously while out for my walk before the tornado. He didn't move but did seem to be regarding us carefully and he kept looking at his wrist, possibly using his personal communications device. We paused as we had done before while the car rose out of the ground. Just as it did so, the Guardian began to walk swiftly and purposefully towards us. He raised his right hand and shouted:

"Stop! By order of The Union you are commanded to cease what you are doing and come with me!"

"Not bloody likely!" I responded and we ran the last few metres to the car and jumped in.

He began to run at full pelt towards us just as the professor slammed his foot on the accelerator and the car sped off at clearly far more than the speed limit.

"It's not all computer controlled you know," he winked conspiratorially, "I simply had to leave some element of human control for emergencies!"

As we accelerated off down the road, I looked in the rear view vision systems, there were now four blue cars in pursuit.

"We've got some people on our tail!" I said.

"I am aware of them," he said grinning. "But it's ok 'cos I have a cunning plan," and waggled an eyebrow enigmatically.

The four cars behind us had now formed a line across the road, preventing anyone from overtaking them and getting in the way. Luckily, there was little traffic and so this did not cause any accidents. They were obviously gaining on us as we drove along the long straight road out of Cambridge, heading towards Wandlebury.

"They're still behind us!" I said as we zoomed around the Addenbrooke's roundabout on two wheels.

"I know!" he said and made an extremely tight right hand turn.

"What the hell are you doing?" I spluttered as I was thrown against the side pillar.

"Just playing a little game with them," he said motioning at the vehicles in the rear view sensor screen.

He then drove through the desolate hospital car park at break-neck speed, driving straight over the divisions between the long abandoned parking spaces.

The car's suspension absorbed the bumps nicely so we barely noticed them. The four Guardian cars in pursuit had now split up, clearly thinking that they could trap us by blocking the escape routes. Within a couple of minutes, they had done just that.

"Erm, Professor, you might want to rethink your plan?" I said warily as we stopped dead in a little access road. The end of which, some fifteen metres away was blocked by a Guardian's car. He grinned back at me.

"Don't worry old chum. You know I said I'd made some modifications to the car?"

"Y..e..s." I said slowly.

"Watch this!" He twisted a small cylindrical device on the dashboard. Nothing happened.

"What's happening?" I asked.

"It's a portable camo drive," he responded.

"Oh, that's rather clever," I said as he put the car in reverse and slowly trundled backwards, away from the road block.

It had obviously worked as the Guardian's cars begun to move again and drove about willy-nilly clearly searching for us. We stopped by a tall hedge and remained stationery while they buzzed around hunting for the vehicle, clearly confused by what had happened. We watched for perhaps a minute and then he restarted the engine and swung the car through a hundred and eight degrees and sped off in the opposite direction grinning to himself. He then pressed another large button on the dashboard and the car rose unsteadily into the air.

"I made this modification too!" he said proudly.

We rose to a height of about five metres and set off back towards the main road. Once on the road, we kept low in order to avoid overhanging trees and obstructions. After a few minutes flight, the professor landed on the pitted surface a short way after the housing petered out at the outer edges of the city. He then continued to drive normally along the road. He did point out that the camo drive was still operational so we would remain invisible. I directed him to the muddy track that led towards the area where I had parked the ship. There was no one about and our only company were a few blackbirds who were singing merrily in the hedgerows. They took flight as we whooshed by but looked rather puzzled by the lack of a visible object to be afraid of.

We stopped near where I had left the ship and I opened the hatch using the button on my belt. The professor fussed about with the car for a couple of minutes, turned off the camo drive, pulled a few levers and pushed a few buttons. The boot popped open and I grabbed our things and ran into the ship while he got out of the car. From the cockpit, I kept watch for anything untoward when a sudden funny whirring noise made me leave the ship. I got to the hatch just in time to see the car begin to collapse in on itself, panels fold and slide into each other and the wheels deflate and retract into the base of the vehicle. I watched open mouthed as what had been a comfortably sized vehicle for two people ended up the size of a large suitcase, complete with four small wheels at the bottom.

"More modifications?" I asked slightly sarcastically.

"Yep!" he replied.

He then pulled out a little handle from the top and dragged the now compacted car into the stern of the ship.

"Right," he said. "So this is your ship?"

"Well," I said conversationally, "technically it's my sister's – she lent me the money to buy it from The Union after I finished my mining service. I've been paying her back for years. She's called *The Cowrie* and I've made a few modifications to her over the years" I said proudly, "She has upgraded weapon systems and I pinched a camo drive from a Union ship on Ventos. I upgraded the power grid too so despite the new systems, there is no power drain."

"Hmm," he said and put his head on one side. "What about the engines – how d'you account for the power weight ratio distribution changes with the additional weight?"

"I didn't, I have however noted that there is a slight alteration in maximum velocity but it's not sufficient to cause me any major problems unless..."

"I'm...being...chased...by...someone...who...erm...wishes……..me...erm..."
My brain finally caught up with the situation that I now found myself in.

"Shit." I said flatly.

"No matter," said the professor matter of factly. "Let's have a look at the power distribution manifold and see if I can't help you."

With that, he grabbed a few tools from the kit on the wall and strode off towards the back of the ship. As he walked down the ramp, he called:

"Don't start her up just yet, let me finish tinkering. Shouldn't be very long."

The professor was true to his word and ten minutes later he emerged panels housing the engine mechanisms, smiling and covered in grime. He strolled up the ramp and made his way to the cockpit where I was just finishing off making a cup of Tealog. I quickly offered him a mug.

"Thanks," he said sipping his drink. "Should be ok now, I just rerouted the primary fuel lines through the central manifold and inverted the directional array. Really simple change actually. Your power output should be something in the order of one hundred and twenty percent compared to before. I don't know why more people don't do that on these ships, it's no great effort."

"Ok" I said slowly. "So can I start her up now?"

"Sure, go for it – just be a little careful on the throttle as you've got additional power and so your rate of climb will be much improved compared to before."

I had a final swig of Tealog, settled into the chair, waited while the professor sat in the other chair in front of the weapons console and strapped himself in. I then started the engines and was immediately struck by the power as I struggled to avoid losing control.

"Blimey!" I said as the joystick wobbled furiously. "That's amazing!"

I set the autopilot and let the ship hover about ten metres off the ground. Luckily this system seemed to be able to handle the additional power with no problems whatsoever.

"Ok, where to then?" I asked eager to know what his plan was.

"The Union has a headquarters for RnD just outside Derby, in Mickleover. That's probably where your little green alien friend is being held. But, if you wanted to be sure, you could turn on the infrasonic detection systems and see if you can pick up his signal."

"Ah, good idea," I said and opened the communication systems control subroutine on the main panel. I stared at the screen for a few seconds, muttering under my breath as I negotiated the complex menus. After a couple of minutes, I found it but I got the feeling from the professor's harrumphing and murmuring thought he probably could have done it far more quickly.

I looked at the display, there was a faint signal ping one hundred and three kilometres away.

"Great, so the FPO is still alive!" I said happily.

"Looks like it." replied the professor smiling broadly, looking over my shoulder.

I sat back in my chair, programmed in the course, switched on the camo drive, turned off the autopilot and engaged the suborbital engines. The ship leapt forward at a terrific rate.

"We'll be there in a few moments with this additional speed, thanks for doing that." I said proudly.

"Pah, think nothing of it, my old chum!" he replied and grinned.

Within a quarter of an hour we were flying over the centre of Derby westwards towards Mickleover. The city had undergone a massive regeneration in the early 21st century but since the death of much of the population of the country, it was now largely deserted like almost all large cities around the world. It was a shame to see so much dereliction in what had once been a thriving area. The railway line was all but obliterated by trees but the route it used to follow was still faintly visible. Much of the road system was still there but the surfaces of the roads, even viewed from a height of ten metres were visibly cracked and in need of maintenance. One of the overpasses had collapsed and a large "No Entry" sign had been placed clumsily across it. I guessed no one had wanted to go that way for a very long time. As we approached Mickleover in silence, I could see a large dome-like structure like the one on Ventos – this was obviously a favourite architectural style of The Union. It was slightly larger than the one on Ventos and much more heavily defended, if the gun turrets and small patrol ships which showed up on the sensors were anything to go by.

Flying low to the ground, I brought the ship in to land in a quiet abandoned cul-de-sac just off the main road that led to the dome. We were two kilometres away by road but it was potentially dangerous to get any closer even with a camo drive due to the patrols and the occasional Guardian car that we'd observed on the road during out flight.

After a quick lunch and more Tealog, we left the ship. It was early afternoon by now and the weather here was a little less settled than it had been in Cambridgeshire. The sun was now and again obscured by thin high cloud and I had noted while we were in the air some very large anvil shaped cumulonimbus clouds building in the distance off to the west – it looked like we might well be in for another huge storm. We'd not had any of the communications channels turned on during the flight for fear of detection so had had no warning of any potentially bad weather in the Midlands. Nonetheless, it was quite pleasantly warm as we marched along the road. As we made our way inexorably towards the dome, there were regular patrols but these were easy to avoid as there were plenty of hiding places amongst the rubble and abandoned dwellings. There was a checkpoint set up one kilometre from the dome and we observed it uneasily from behind a long since abandoned hedge. I took out my polyscope. There were four heavily armed Guardians holed up behind a large barricade with the traditional barrier across the road. They looked fierce, even from this distance and a full head on confrontation with them would definitely alert The Union to our presence, plus we'd probably get killed in the process. We needed a plan.

        After a few seconds thought, the professor stood up.

"Follow my lead," he said quietly and walked out from behind the hedge, heading directly for the barricade. It wasn't long before one of the guards spotted him and shouted:

"Halt!" he yelled in a field voice. "This is a restricted area for RnD Union personnel only. Stop immediately or you will be shot!"

"It's ok," he said stopping and loudly raising his hands, "I'm Professor Karl McDoughale of Cambridge University. I wanted to have a look at your RnD facilities – I have a pass," he said, brandishing a fist sized piece of bioplastic which he'd removed from his jacket inside pocket. The Guardian walked warily up to him all the time pointing his evil looking rifle at him. He snatched the card and returned to his booth where he slotted it into a card reader and peered at the tiny screen beside it. The other Guardians remained at their posts with their guns trained on us both.

"Yes, you are who you say you are," he said a few seconds later. "But who's this?" he asked pointing at me accusingly.

"This is my prisoner, Paul Heath." he said calmly. "He's trying to take down The Union. I thought I'd better bring him in and this was the nearest large Union outpost to Cambridge. He's wanted for treason and destruction of Union property, amongst other things. He also knows a lot about the classified Union mining operation on Ventos. I think some intensive interrogation might help answer some of our questions about that planet."
The Guardian smiled evilly and said "Sleeve."

The professor looked puzzled for a millisecond and then rolled up his left sleeve to reveal another one of the mind control bracelets. I stood there shocked for a few seconds but he turned his head slightly and managed to wink surreptitiously at me.

"Right then." said the Guardian matter of factly, peering at me. "I believe he's on today's list of wanted felons. Thanks for bringing him in Professor, you will be rewarded accordingly."
He then hit me in the stomach with the butt of his gun and I collapsed into a heap on the floor.

"Get up!" he yelled.
I gasped and stood up carefully.
I was grabbed by two of the remaining Guardians and manhandled into the booth. A large needle was jabbed into my arm and a DNA sample was taken and slotted into a portable DNA reader which stood in the corner of the small room. After a few seconds it beeped and the Guardian confirmed my identity.

"Gotya" he said. "Tollie, take him to the prison in the dome, he's got some explaining to do before we execute him."

The other Guardian, whose name was obviously Tollie, nodded and motioned me towards a patrol car with the dangerous end of his gun. He was slightly above average height and slim with a permanent sneer plastered across his face.

"Get in." he growled menacingly.
I obliged and, as I sat in the back of the car, twin restraints popped out from the seats and wound themselves around my wrists and thighs so I was completely immobilised. The professor then climbed in beside me and made himself comfortable. I noted with some displeasure that he wasn't restrained in the same way as I was. I looked at him questioningly but he winked conspiratorially back at me as we sped off down the road. Within seconds, the imposing dome filled the whole of the windscreen. Small anti-aircraft gun posts were situated at regular intervals up the sides of it and every

few seconds a small remote controlled scout ship, like those I had destroyed on Ventos, buzzed across it. I felt nauseous, partly due to fear but also due to being hit in the stomach so soon after having had lunch.

Within a short space of time, we were at the entrance to the dome. This opened automatically as the vehicle approached. On either side were two booths, similar to the one I'd just been in and all manned by Guardian personnel with guns. They were unsmiling and fierce looking and had the look of people who would happily use their weapons just for a laugh. As the vehicle drew to a stop outside the main compound entrance, my restraints retracted back in to the seats and, as the door opened, I was grabbed and dragged out of the car by Tollie.
"C'mon. Get inside. Now!" he growled.
I was practically flung at the door of the compound while the professor was directed off to the main RnD building opposite. Tollie followed as I was led down the main corridor. There were several Guardians milling about looking bored but news of my arrival had clearly got around as they perked up when they saw me, cursing and mocking me as I was pushed unceremoniously down the gloomy corridor. There were numerous grey coloured doors off on either side.

"I'm really sorry," said Tollie in a sarcastic tone of voice which indicated that he wasn't at all sorry, "our penthouse is fully booked so you'll have to go in here" –

he typed in a six digit passcode and a metal door opened in front of us. He pointed into the gloomy space which was a small square cell with no windows and the obligatory revolting looking toilet on one wall. As I hesitated on the threshold, he pushed me hard in the small of my back and I fell in, face first, landing painfully on the floor. The door slammed behind me, cutting out the jeering and mocking from the Guardians who were stood outside.

I stood up slowly and surveyed the area. The cell was about five metres square with a bench on one side, a hessian mat which presumably served as a bed opposite and the toilet on the other wall. The wall with the door in it had no other distinguishing features aside from the usual clock above the door. 'Homely', I thought to myself as I settled down on the bed. I pulled my knees up to my chest and waited to see what would happen next. A few moments later, a small trapdoor opened up in the door and a cup of liquid was thrust in on a small tray. I stood up and grabbed it off the tray which then retracted back into the door. Despite the risks of a truth serum or a drug, I was glad of the drink as I had grown thirsty. Unfortunately, it was probably the most disgusting cup of Tealog that I had ever drunk. They had hugely overdone the tannin levels and they'd not even bothered to put sugar in it. Nonetheless, I drank it quickly and left it beside the door. I returned to my spot on the bed, curled up in to a ball and thought. It was all very well the professor saying that he had a "plan" and to "follow his lead" but that left me completely in the dark and so here I was, locked up in a dingy cell with who knows how many angry trigger happy Guardians outside. I also wondered about several things which had happened - how come he had two bracelets on, one on each side? Even more confusingly, why had he winked at me - was he actually still under the mind controlling influence of the metal or not? I considered this for a few moments but couldn't find and answer so gave up, closed my eyes and then drifted off into an uncharacteristic mid-afternoon doze. My last thought was that maybe the Tealog had been laced with a sedative after all.

    I don't know how long it was before the door exploded off its hinges and woke me up. It must have been some considerable time later as the light levels in the corridor had dropped appreciably. It was either going dark or the nasty looking storms I had seen forming earlier were nearby - not that that should matter as we were underneath a dome. I lay on the bed for a while, feeling a little spaced out. My mouth was very dry and I had a revolting taste in my mouth. My head felt unaccountably fuzzy and my vision was slightly off too. I took a few deep breaths, waited for my vision to clear and struggled upright. After a few minutes, I decided that I was slightly woozy but none the worse for it. I stood up carefully and cautiously approached the ravaged door and looked out into the corridor. There was no sign of any Guardians, jeering or otherwise and the only sounds were my own breathing and the sound of cooling metal from the door that lay crumpled in a heap in the middle of my cell.

    I checked again in both directions, just to be sure, and then set off towards the main entrance of the building. I couldn't run as I didn't feel up to it so I jogged along the corridor keeping my eyes open for anyone. I needn't have worried as there was no one around. What the hell was going on? I reached the entrance of the building and gently pushed open the main doors. Opposite was the building which the professor had gone into but this now looked like a bomb had gone off within it – the doors were hanging off the hinges and smoke was billowing from several of the shattered windows. In the distance, on the far edge of the dome I could see people running around in abject terror and their cries echoed strangely around the enclosed space. I stood there for a few seconds before a familiar sounding voice called across to me from behind an overturned car.

    "Paul, over here!"

I forced myself to run towards the car and found the professor lurking behind it, hunkered down close to the ground.

    "What's going on?" I asked.

    "Not exactly sure, I tinkered about with their computer a bit and set off the fire alarms to get everyone out, including you. I also disabled the weapons grid, deactivated the defence perimeter and the structural integrity field. Then I had a proper look around while you were incarcerated. Sorry about that, I had to get them to trust me."

"Where did you get the other bracelet from?" I asked.

"Oh, it's a fake. I wondered if they might check so I thought it was best to take extra precautions."

"Glad you did."

"Hmm, me too. Now, let's find your little green friend, shall we?"

"Yep," I replied "but how – this complex is massive?"

"I've rigged up an infrasound detector to my chronometer so we should be able to find it easily."

"Righto!" I replied, impressed.

We set off across the compound, following the direction indicated by the signal, hiding in between short bursts of running. By now I was feeling more human and I felt better with every step that I took. There was no one about now as whatever sabotage he'd done had really worked very effectively. He directed me towards the Research and Development building which was located further over the other side of the dome, on the left hand side. The door was intact here and there was a key card access pad which let us in with his security pass without any bother. The main corridor was deserted. On the right hand side, through some enormous double doors was the biggest lab I'd ever seen. It was more like the size of an old fashioned aircraft hangar. We entered and gawped at the space. The area was stuffed with hundreds of different pieces of scientific equipment, mass spectrophotometers, uHPLCs, GCs, scanners of all sorts and assorted telescopes, mirrors, lasers and biological control apparatus, plus other things that I had no idea what they did. After wondering around for a few moments, we found, over in one corner, breeding pens labelled as being for aardvarks and goats, both seemed really out of place. I wondered if The Union had been through my TBR pile and thought aardvarks were significant in some way.

We continued to search diligently and followed the directions indicated by the pings from the device on the professor's wrist. After a few moments, the sound indicated that the FPO was in the room next door to the unfurnished one in which we now stood. All we could determine was that it was a small room with frosted plated glass windows and another security pass on the door. The professor's pass let us in to a stage III containment facility. We walked past the area for the containment suits and straight into the lab. In the middle was a dissecting table with all the nasty looking instruments you'd expect and, beside that was a plastic cage containing a lot of dirt. There was a line of what looked like Christmas tree lights tied around the top of the cage so I called over the professor. He pondered them carefully for a few seconds, scanned them with his portable chronometer and then stood back, head on one side and hands on his hips.

"It looks like some sort of infrasound dampening field," he mused.

"Ah!" I exclaimed "Maybe that's how they managed to kidnap it in Cambridge without it going postal at them."

He nodded sagely and then ripped them off the edge of the case in one fluid movement.

"Not a problem anymore!" he replied and smiled at me cheerily.

I peered into the box again, I couldn't be sure but it certainly looked very like soil from Ventos. I made a small questioning squeaking noise as I looked downwards. The dirt shifted slightly and, to my immense joy, the FPO rose from the depths of the tank. It looked a little different now. The scarring on its back was more pronounced and it was a little larger. It was also less green than it had been. It looked as if the green had been extracted as each area which lacked colour had a small round two to three millimetre scar in the centre.

"Hello," I said in the special voice I reserved for talking to pets and small children, "what have they been doing to you?"

My question was met with a high pitched series of squeaks punctuated by small pauses. Once it stopped,

I stroked the clearly terrified animal until it seemed slightly calmer and then picked it up and let it snuggle into my hands. I spoke soothingly to it and, after a while, it had calmed down and had stopped trembling.

The professor had been mucking about with the equipment and computers elsewhere in the lab and once I had secured the now calm FPO away in my pocket, I strolled over to talk to him.

"I've had a look at what they're doing," he said excitedly as he looked up at me from a large screen. "They're planning to harvest your little friend for his chloroplasts – they are ninety eight percent more efficient that anything else that we have on this planet. Once they've replicated them, they can use them in bioreactors to generate energy for the whole planet. Unfortunately, they'd need to kill it to get them all and to ensure they have enough for the whole world, they are now planning a return to Ventos to hunt down and capture the remainder of his species."

"Johnsons." I said coldly. "That's not fair. They can't do that!"

"They can and they will," he replied. "The ship is planning to return to Ventos within the week. If we are going to stop them, we need to do something quickly."

"Right," I said. "In that case let's get out there and stop them!"

We left the RnD block in a hurry. The professor insisted that he "borrow" a few bits he'd found in the lab and so was slowed down by the backpack and bagfuls of equipment he'd pinched. I had to practically drag him away. I insisted I take two of them to lighten his load. He reluctantly agreed. Outside, overhead a massive storm was in progress and lightning flashed around giving a very strange appearance to the buildings. Strange lights danced around as ball lightning materialised on either side of the dome and the electromagnetic disturbances caused my ears to ring.

"This is going to be a really colossal storm," I remarked to the professor as we neared the exit.

"I know," he said thoughtfully. "I really don't think under a dome, even if it's a Faraday cage, is particularly safe, to be honest. Especially as I decoupled and depolarised all the structural integrity systems," he said and grinned evilly.

As if in response, a gigantic forked lightning bolt smashed into the dome and a small crack appeared. A not inconsiderable amount of debris rained down around us.

"Let's get the hell out of here!" I yelled as another lightning strike smashed into the dome, creating an interesting arcing effect between the two points as the electrostatic charges persisted at both sites.

We ran, scrambled and tripped our way towards the exit. The guards had all left and their booths were empty. I managed to grab a rifle from the gun rack which had unwisely been left unguarded. I grabbed a spare one for the professor as his hands were full and we headed off out through the front of the dome and in the direction of the checkpoint. By now, the rain and hail were lashing down in torrents and it was hard to see far ahead of us.

"Have you ever fired one of these?" I yelled at the professor in-between gasps as we ran.

"Nope. Shouldn't be too hard to figure out though!" he shouted back with his trademark cheerfulness.

"Wait!" he commanded. He stopped briefly, pointed the gun at a small pile of rubble and pressed the trigger. The pile vaporised immediately as a flash of greenish light hit it. We both stood there, open mouthed.

"Bloody hell," I said. "That's dangerous!"
He nodded in agreement, furrowing his brow. "Let's try not to get shot by one of these then, eh?" Grinning again he continued: "I've never seen weaponry as advanced as this before, most interesting."

We set off again, running towards the area where we'd left the ship. Ahead was the booth where we'd last encountered the guards. It was now deserted but with good reason, as a direct lightning strike appeared to have totally destroyed the building leaving only a burning, smoking shell with no windows or doors. I looked upwards and noticed an ominous bulge in the underside of one of a massive, evil looking black cloud perhaps indicating that a funnel cloud was forming. There was also no sign of the Guardians who had inhabited it only a few hours ago. Perhaps they had noticed the weather and left. After all, if a tornado was due, who wants to get thrown around like sardines in a washing machine?

Beyond the booth lay the road and not far from that, the ship, parked in the central area of the cul-de-sac. We paused again to draw breath and I looked back at the dome, barely visible in the distance due to the storm. I watched stunned as an enormous funnel cloud descended from the sky and slammed into it, just as a huge bolt of lightning struck the opposite side of the structure. Even over the wind and rain, we heard a terrible groaning sound as the structure deformed under the terrific stresses and collapsed inwards. Within seconds, it was pulled up into the spinning, whirling tower of darkness and lost forever. It was a bit childish but I grinned, gave it the two fingers up sign and shouted something very derogatory at it. It seemed fitting. Luckily the professor didn't notice any of this as he was wheezing and trying to catch his breath with his back to me. He looked across at me, smiled vaguely and gave me a thumbs up signal and we continued our progress back toward the ship.

As we rounded the corner near the abandoned cul-de-sac, something stuck me as not quite right. I grabbed the professor's arm as he rounded the corner behind me and pulled him into the safety of an abandoned garage that was missing the door. The wind had subsided by now and the tornado had coiled neatly back up into the clouds. Despite this, the winds were still gusty and the sky was still full of clouds and the rain and hail still fell, albeit much less intensely than earlier on. However, the lightning had still not abated and every so often large rumbles of ominous thunder echoed around the sky. We crouched down in the corner of the garage to talk. The ship itself was screened off by a large overgrown hedge.

"I think we're being watched," I said as quietly as I could in between the swirls of wind, rain and the thunder.

"Hmm. Maybe," he said noncommittally.

I picked up an empty container that was lying disused beside me and flung it as hard as I could out into the open area near the ship. Almost immediately, it was riddled with laser fire.

"Looks like it," he said as the fragments of the container sprayed merrily around the area.

"How come they can see the ship?" I asked.

"No idea." Then he paused.

"But I suppose..." and paused again, thinking it through before answering, "they might have found a hack around the camo drive because you nicked one of theirs so they'd know what frequency it was using."

"Bollocks. That seems plausible though. I should really have thought of that." I said dejectedly.

He didn't answer immediately and scratched his head thoughtfully. "Let's see if we can't find a way around this." he said positively.
He pointed to the adjoining door between the garage and the house, just visible in the half light.

"If we sneak through the house, we'll have less distance to cover to get to the ship so we stand a better chance of not getting shot at."

I nodded in approval and we made our way as carefully as possible towards the door. The house had clearly been abandoned for a long time and leaves and debris had piled up inside the garage but it was no problem to make our way to the door. It was stuck fast but a couple of brisk charges with my shoulder took care of it and we entered the house. Inside, the door through which we had entered was now behind us and in front was a large dining room. Illuminated by the lightning, a large and rather impressive wooden table inlaid with nice swirly patterns was ahead and beyond that was another door to a kitchen area. We tiptoed around the table and entered the kitchen. This too contained another decorative table and all of the usual domestic appliances, none of which looked to be still in working order. A very unpleasant stale smell hung in the air. We said nothing as we stealthily made our way to the back door which was open and had let in leaves, twigs and other debris from outside. The garden was long and narrow and once maybe been mostly given over to turf but was now full of brambles and overgrown shrubs. At the bottom end just visible through the jungle, was a greenhouse, long fallen into disuse. Most of the panels were smashed and the metal certainly shouldn't have been the colour that it was. To our left was a small passage which led along the side of the house, out towards the road and the back of the ship. It ended with a rather ornate metallic gate which had long since gone completely rusty and seemed to be held together with the spider's webs that adorned it. We crept along the passage in complete silence and I peered around the corner through the filigree pattern. Sure enough, in the front garden of the house opposite, there was a Guardian sniper, trying rather unsuccessfully to hide behind a statue of a small boy having a wee – he looked like the one who'd kicked me into my cell earlier on. Behind him in the darkness I could just make out another three disreputable looking Guardians all of whom were heavily armed and looked like they intended to kill anyone who got in their way. We scuttled back from the end of the passage.

"We're pinned down professor, what would you suggest? There's no way we can get to the ship without getting shot."

The professor thought for a moment and then, in between the howling of the wind he explained one of the things that he'd stolen from the dome.

"It's a high frequency stun grenade," he said. "I raided their weapons research lab as well as ruining their AI systems. All you need to do is lob it out into the area and let it go off. It will incapacitate anyone who is looking at it. One of their weapons specialists was kind enough to explain to me what it is and how it works. She boasted that it would be useful for quelling the increased levels on unrest against The Union."

"Ok," I answered carefully. "So how do I get their attention?"

"I'm sure you'll find a way but once you've thrown it, just be sure to close your eyes tightly and cover your ears. It'll be fine," he added reassuringly.

I thought about it for a few seconds, I had no choice whatsoever but to undertake this crazy plan.

I waited until a lull in the weather and then stuck my arm out and yelled:

"Oi! Dickheads!" and threw the grenade out into the green space that lay just in front of the currently invisible ship.

I then shut my eyes hard and shoved my fingers into my ears and ducked back into the alleyway.

There was an explosion and then silence. After a few seconds, I looked out. There was no movement. I picked up a stone and threw it out into the path of the guns. Nothing happened.

"How long do we have?" I asked cautiously.

"About a minute, I think," he replied.

"Great," I said grabbed his arm, all the bags of stolen equipment and dragged him quickly to the ship's entrance. The ramp extended and we jumped on board. The whole process took maybe forty five seconds and just

as the trapdoor closed, the laser fire began. The armoured plating absorbed the laser bolts rather effectively and they bounced harmlessly off, randomly destroying a bit of one of the houses and causing a rather unpleasant injury to the statue of the small boy having a pee.
I ran up to the cockpit.

"Let's get out of here!" I exclaimed.

"We can't," he answered coolly.

"Why?"

"The storm. Any attempt to take off in these cross winds and lighting would be almost impossible and potentially fatal. Best to wait it out here."

"Are you out of your mind? I have done this sort of thing before!" I responded angrily.

"No. I'm being practical," he replied carefully.

"Look," I retorted. "There are a bunch of heavily armed bastards out there who want to kill me and you suggest that we stay here like a pair of sitting ducks?"

"Yes."

"Stuff that! I've flown in worse than this and I do actually know what the fuck I'm doing!" I said stridently and ran back into the cockpit.

"Don't be stupid Paul, there is no way that you can navigate through that storm." he called pointing out into the night as, right on cue, an especially vicious fork of lightning stuck a nearby tree and set it on fire, despite the rain.

The Ventos Conspiracy 2

In all my time alone on Ventos and quite a lot of it since, I was used to making decisions on my own so the millisecond he was on board, I had slumped into the captain's chair. Once he'd noticed my determined expression and complained bitterly, he reluctantly strapped himself in. I wrenched the control stick forwards and powered up the engines. The ship rose unsteadily but rapidly into the air. I adjusted the course accordingly and fought to control it as the wind blasted from left to right. I gasped as the left wing of the ship pitched viciously towards the roof of one of the houses. I pulled up just in time and corrected for the drag from the atmosphere just as a series of laser blasts impacted harmlessly on the rear end of the ship. As we flew off unsteadily into the dark, I turned back to the professor and said:

"Don't worry, I got this! We're not going far – just enough to get out of the range of these Guardians."

I flew us slowly and erratically back towards the city centre, struggling to control the ship. There was a large area of forest situated in the middle that I had noticed on the way over and I aimed for that as it seemed like a good area to hide in. Scanners detected that it had a large clearing in the middle so there was space to land safely. Landing in these cross winds was not easy but I'd had plenty of practise on Ventos and we settled down in the north west corner of the park, not far from an overgrown and abandoned children's play area. I turned round and spoke to the professor.

"See, told you" I said boastfully, "I think we'll be safe here, at least for now."
He mumbled something unintelligible in reply. I ignored him and looked at the camo drive I had hastily installed back on Ventos. I'd kept the original one in the storage area at the back of the ship and it didn't take long to swap them back over so The Union wouldn't be able to detect us in the way that they had apparently done so before. Once disconnected from the ship's power supply, it would be completely inert.

"That should help." I said quietly.
"Hmm," he replied moodily.

Only after that was done did I retrieve the FPO from my pocket. It had remained quiet and still for the whole last few hours but happily jumped back into the dirt box and quickly buried itself. I turned the UV lamps on and left it to recover properly. The poor thing had obviously been prodded and poked about and injured so would need time to recuperate. I felt very protective towards it, it had, after all, saved my life on more than one occasion and it was my fault for bringing it to Earth so I felt responsible for its suffering.

We dug out the rations while the storm continued to rage outside and had a pretty decent meal. Luckily, there were no further tornados and a while after we'd finished eating, the storm had all but subsided. Hopefully, we would soon be able to resume our journey to The Union headquarters. Once the professor had calmed down, we had a short discussion about what to do, we weren't that far from the Guardians and so it would be sensible not to linger for too long. However, it was now properly dark and night flying was forbidden by the Union which presented us with an issue. It suddenly dawned on me that we could drive instead. It wasn't a feature I had used before - I always used public transport for work (as directed by The Union) and on the rare occasions I had to go out not for work purposes, I preferred to walk. It did require some external modifications to be made in order to change it into a ground going vehicle but, with the two of us working on it, it wouldn't take long. Despite all of the assorted alterations that I had made, I had kept the basic underlying systems were unchanged so it was still perfectly possible to convert it.

    I dug out the well-thumbed manual from the underside of the main console to find out how. Looking at the index, I found the relevant section and opened the very thick book at the correct pages. I gawped at it for a few seconds then turned it upside down and then sideways and scratched my head thoughtfully. It still made no sense.

    "Professor?" I asked sheepishly. "I can't make head nor tail of these diagrams."

"Let me have a look." He said, putting his glass of Rioja down on the laboratory table beside him.

"Blimey!" he exclaimed. "I can see why. Even the text is gibberish! Is it in Latin do you think?"

"I don't think so," I replied. "Looks more like Martian."

He stifled a slightly tipsy sounding giggle and then peered at it again.

"The diagrams are so poor, they look like they've been drawn by someone who couldn't draw for toffee, and probably couldn't even draw actual toffee either."

We laughed at this and it seemed ease our annoyance with each-other from earlier on. We spent the next fifteen minutes scrutinising the diagrams and text. Eventually the professor stood up and said:

"Right. I think I know what we have to do now. Follow me."

We walked towards the rear of the ship and on the way, grabbed a toolkit and a couple of head torches. We checked the coast was clear and then exited the ship and walked out into the darkness. The wind and rain had stopped now and the sky was partly clear with a few ragged looking clouds scudding over the three quarter moon. The ground was a morass of mud beneath our feet and the whole area smelled of damp vegetation and decay.

"Ok..." he said slowly. "If, and I do mean if, I am reading this right, if we undo these retaining bolts just behind the main engines and remove these bits here and here," he pointed at the totally inadequate diagram in the book, illuminated by the head torch, "then we should be ok. I think."

He passed me a wrench and I wandered around to the starboard rear engine. The bolt was absolutely stuck fast and refused to move. Another quick search in the toolbox produced an ancient can of WD-50 so this was sprayed liberally over the bolt. After several minutes of persistent effort, the thing finally moved. I then moved around to the other side and tried the same procedure with the other bolt. Luckily, that one was far easier. The professor then walked round to the other side of the ship and held onto the supporting bar while we simultaneously unscrewed the bolts the last few turns. We then lifted the large metal drive plate clear, it was incredibly light for its size and we easily manoeuvred it round and put it safely in the hold.

We stood back to admire our handiwork and then climbed back on board. The second phase of the transformation of the ship was to press a few buttons and pull a few levers so required far less effort. The hardest part of the operation was actually finding the lever to initialise the axles as it was right underneath the control console in the gloom. However, with some shining of torches, we were able to see it and figure out which way to turn it. There was a loud grinding sound accompanied by some nasty higher frequency noises which presumably meant that the wheels were moving. That done, there was a loud "clunk" as they locked in place. I then looked under the main console and found the relevant controls to decouple the energy conduits for the main engines and reroute them to the driveshaft. Lastly, the wings then retracted into the fuselage automatically and I waited a couple more minutes for everything to align correctly and then returned to the cockpit and started the engines. The efficiency of these would be much lower due to the additional friction of driving on roads however all we needed to do was get clear of the city and then we could stop and fly the rest of the way to Poland and stop The Union.

Chapter five – A Polish interlude

The only things impeding our journey were the trees surrounding the clearing. However, we did have some mining lasers at the front of the ship which in a very short space of time very efficiently cleared a path, wide enough for us to drive out. The nearest main road that would be sufficiently wide to drive down without destroying large quantities of semi derelict houses was a left turn out of the park and back to a T-junction and going then right. This would lead to the main road and out of the city. This would initially take us in the wrong direction for heading towards Poland but it was necessary. This was a much simpler route so we bumped over the kerbstones and drove onto the road. There was no one else about. I drove slowly at first as, even with the camo drive running, there was still a chance of detection due to the sound of the engines. The road itself had seen better days, tree roots and leaves were pooled in the extensive potholes which had opened up as The Union had withdrawn support from much of the country. This was one of the main reasons for the unrest in the Midlands and the North as, even more than in the 20th and 21st centuries, the south east centred view of the country was very prevalent and was reflected in every aspect of life.

We reached the end of the road and turned smartly left, onto a road which the navigational system told us was called Queensway, a dual carriageway. As we drove along, here and there were still a few indications that people lived and worked here. Once out on the open road, we accelerated quickly away from the city and out into open country. Many of the overpasses had been removed decades ago which was convenient due to the height of the ship. It was actually a pleasant drive, even in the dark. After an hour, having driven through Nottingham and turning south onto the old M1, crossing over the River Trent and heading off towards Leicester, we stopped in an abandoned motorway service station and fell asleep.

I awoke some hours later. Through the front screen of the ship, I could see that the sun was just edging over the horizon and the sky was an exquisite clear pale blue colour. There was no sign whatsoever of the dreadful weather of the previous day. The external sensors indicated that it was a warm morning and so I roused myself from the uncomfortable chair, stretched, yawned and woke the professor up. He was initially ambivalent towards the idea of waking up but, when presented with a large mug of Tealog and breakfast, he brightened considerably. By this stage, the sun was a few degrees off the horizon and the day was warming up nicely.

Upon further investigation of the hieroglyphics in the manual, we discovered that it was far simpler to modify the ship back to aerial mode than to change it to terrestrial mode so it was the work of a few moments to make it airworthy again. Once that was done, I started the main engines and launched the ship high into the stratosphere, it was quicker and far more fuel efficient this way than ploughing through the thicker lower layers of the atmosphere and there was also a smaller chance of being detected. The flight distance was approximately one thousand five hundred kilometres so, flying at a thousand kilometres an hour, we would be there in about one and a half hours. This way, I would not overtax the engines and we could charge the ship's power supply *en route* as we would be above the level of the clouds.

The flight to central Poland was uneventful and we landed safely near the town of Bełchatów in a quiet forest clearing about ten kilometres from our target. The base was clearly on high alert as from low orbit we were able to detect a lot of audio traffic and there were a plenty of Guardian patrols visible as we descended through the cloud layers. The base was located in what had once been the largest open cast coal mine in Poland. Much of the power requirements for the base were generated by the heavily upgraded power station which was right beside it. In the early 21st century, the coal mine had closed and had been, at one time, referred to locally as "The Big Hole". Once The Union took over, this enormous crater had been filled in with the inner workings of the organisation and then covered over in the usual fashion. Also visible from the ship as we flew in, beside the dome, was a large area which was presumably used as a lift off point for spaceships. There was nothing on it at present but in the next few days, a ship would be launching to travel to Ventos and harvest the FPOs.

We gathered our gear, camouflaged the ship and walked out into the thick evergreen forest. I tucked the FPO safely into the small pocket located at the top of the backpack so that it could "see" out and catch some sunlight. We both had backpacks but the professor insisted in bringing his car which I told him repeatedly was unnecessary. He ignored me and lugged it along anyway. He brought quite a few bits and pieces that he'd stolen but some things I managed to persuade him to leave behind on the ship. He reluctantly stowed them away for later.

We walked quickly and silently through the thick forest, heading towards the perimeter fence. Most of our route was through a huge tract of trees which provided very good cover until we got close enough to break through the fence. There was no one about at all and the only sounds were the creak of the trees in the breeze and the occasional chirruping of birds. One especially loud noise spooked me and when I looked at the professor for answers he said:

"It's ok, it's probably just pigeons f – ighting" He paused after the "f" in fighting in an attempt to lighten the mood, which it did and we laughed for a couple of moments before continuing.

There were no patrols anywhere and our progress was quick, despite the uneven terrain. We kept up a vigorous pace and were soon in a position where we could see the fence line, about fifty metres away. It would have been foolish to convert *The Cowrie* to terrestrial mode as the last thing we wanted to do was to attract unwelcome attention by turning up in a honking great vehicle, armed to the teeth - they would know we were here soon enough. We were on the north western edge of the base as scans from the air had determined this was the least well-guarded area.

In order to gain access to the base, it did mean a short swim as the intervening space was occupied with a pond which had formed as the smaller satellite excavations away from the main pit had filled with water. Some of these had names and had been used as pleasure parks for the locals but these were all abandoned now as The Union had enclosed them within its arena. The pair of us stepped quietly into the pond, holding our rucksacks above our heads. It turned out that it was only about a metre deep so it only came up about three quarters of the way up my thighs. The professor, being considerably shorter than I, got quite a bit wetter. After a short, wet walk, we got to the fence, hunkered down in a hollow and allowed our shoes, trousers and stockinged feet to dry slightly in the warm sunshine all the while keeping an eye out for company.

Behind us was the fence, standing four metres high and made of metallic links, joined together. It hummed gently in the warm summer air.
"Electrified," murmured the professor quietly.
"I guessed so." I said. "Any ideas?"
He did not respond but pulled out a length of superconducting filament from the backpack and donned a pair of rubber anti electrostatic gloves. He spread the filament out and carefully attached all the loose ends to one of the larger metal poles which supported the deadly metallic mesh. Then he attached the other end to the next metal pole three metres away so that we were enclosed in an electrical bubble. Once the circuit was completed, the current would now flow along the filament, rather than just the fence. Next, he checked it with the scanner to be was sure it was ok and nodded. Lastly, he removed a portable laser from the backpack and severed the links in the fence on both sides, completing the door by slicing horizontally through the links at about head height. The flow of electrons would be uninterrupted as the charge flowed around us and the fence would register as unbroken in the control centre. We stood back and watched as the section of separated

fence fell backwards with a dismal sounding 'flop' on the grass beyond.

"There you go, all safe now," he said beaming cheerfully.

We stepped through the portal and looked across the landscape. It was a gently undulating set of hills, covered in tussocks of grass with occasional hollows which looked muddier. The general angle of the ground was upwards so hopefully we should be able to get to a point where we could survey the base before attempting to get inside. The wind blew gently towards us as we started to make our way up the hill. Large dragonflies buzzed around in the summer air, bees flew merrily around and pollinated the many wildflowers which grew on the plain. There were also a few birds around, calling loudly to one another across the grasslands. If it wasn't all so dangerous, it would have been a very pleasant summer stroll in the country.

As predicted, the small hills came to a stop so we lay on the grass and looked over the edge. Before us was another flat area of land, this time sloping gently downwards towards "The Big Hole" and the dome which enclosed the buildings. The land here was drier and it looked as though it had been interfered with in some way. It occurred to me that this had, so far, been far too easy and something didn't seem right. Puzzled, I pulled out the handheld scanner, linked it to the polyscope and scanned the area downhill of our location. Unsurprisingly, it was mined - not with explosives but with electrical minimines which would paralyse and quickly kill anyone who stood on them for long enough. These were generally thought to be a lot less nasty than the explosive equivalent as it was easier to clean up the mess afterwards. However, the end result for the unfortunate victim was invariably paralysis and, more usually, death. The minimines were also very small, planted by robots in a totally random pattern and so it would be nearly impossible to avoid triggering them - we had to find a way around.

Crestfallen, we descended from the crest of the hill the way we had come and walked along for a few minutes, every so often popping our heads over the parapet and scanning to see if the minefield petered out. It hadn't. It was exasperating but there was nothing we could do. Any triggering of the mines would at the very least alert The Union to our presence or kill us both and we were still some way from the nerve centre.

The base was shaped like an eye with a pointed area at both ends, mimicking the shape of "The Big Hole" which it occupied so presumably both sides were equally protected up as far as the main entrance road. We had no choice but to use that as our point of entry which meant we would have to use the car. The professor made a great show of pointing out that he'd been right to lug the suitcase sized device all the way, against my recommendations.

We fell back to a flatter area of land, and he pressed the button on the top of the collapsed car and stood back as it unfolded back into a vehicle shape. The first thing he did was climb in and initialise the camo drive so at least it would be invisible. I took the FPO out from the backpack and placed it on the central console between the driver's seat and the passenger seat. Then I then stowed our gear in the boot but, as I clambered in, I had an idea.

"Professor, is the outer shell of the car metallic?"

"Yes," he said, "mostly."

"Then it should act as a Faraday cage so we can drive over the mines."

"Mmm," he said grudgingly. "It might work. But they will be able to detect us setting them off and send out the guard robots to find us."

"Well," I paused as my brain caught up with my mouth. "in that case can we use the car as a diversion? Could it drive remotely?"

"Yes," he said slowly. "And I believe I can also rig it to overload to make a really impressive distraction that should keep them off our tail for a while. It wasn't that hard to build so I can always make another one when I get back to Cambridge." He added cheerfully.

I removed the FPO from the car, putting it in my knapsack so it could look out at the scenery. Meanwhile, the professor messed about with the engine under the bonnet and then inside with the controls on the console, muttering to himself from time to time. From what I could tell, most of it was cursing The Union mixed in with various theories and physics, only some of which I understood. I turned my attentions back to my little friend, since we had rescued it, it had remained pretty motionless and had barely squeaked at all. I felt sorry for it but I didn't know what else I could do except keep it in the sunlight which it fed upon. It was impossible to determine its mood and it had no way of communicating with me what it wanted so all I could do was make it as comfortable as possible. As the professor worked on the car, I sat down on the grass and spoke calmly to it for a few minutes. It didn't respond but it seemed to appreciate the attention.

A few moments later, the professor tapped me on the shoulder and he explained what he had done.

"That should do it," he said conversationally, "I've told the on-board computer to wait 20 minutes and then drive in a straight line across the minefield towards the dome. When it gets there, which I calculate should take forty five seconds, I have also programmed it to flood the engine compartment with hydrogen by opening the control valves. I've then told it to switch on all the lights simultaneously which will create a spark sufficient to ignite the gas. Obviously, I've overridden all of the safety protocols so I predict that it will explode in a most impressive manner!"

"Great stuff," I replied. "Let's get going!"
We set off back towards the main road.

"So then, do you have a plan for how to get us unseen along the road to the entrance?"

He grinned extra widely and replied, "I'm not sure if I mentioned this but I've also modified the camo drive from the car. It was something I was working on back in Cambridge before you arrived. It should be able to work independently of the car or the ship as I have invented a converter that creates an area of distortion ahead of the individual who is carrying it. The field strength is high enough to create a bubble of invisibility around two people, I calculate it will be about a metre and a half wide and about two and a half metres tall, so there will be plenty of space for us both to hide inside."

He brandished a funny looking piece of equipment in his left hand – It was grey in colour and covered in lots of panels and coloured lights. It thought it looked like a cross between a cheese grater and a toilet brush with a large flat piece at one end with a recess for the car's miniature camo drive to slot into. The camo drive cylinder was in his right hand and then he said:

"All I need to do is plug it into this!" and, with a theatrical flourish, he did so. As before, nothing seemed to happen but from the professor's smug look, it was obvious that it was working.

We walked warily along for a few minutes in complete silence until we reached the road. We trod carefully so as not to kick and stones or make any sign that we were there. Ahead on the road was a patrol, the members of which were stood about looking bored. They didn't even notice as we slipped by on the other side of the road. However, just after we got past them, the professor suppressed a sneeze and one of the guards looked over to where we were standing, stock-still and hardly breathing. He looked away, shook his head and told one of the other guards sarcastically to go and blow his nose.

We kept walking, listening out for the diversion and, just when I was beginning to think that something might have gone wrong, there was an enormous explosion. In unison, we turned round just in time to see a bright orange flame rising into the blue sky along the side of the dome. The dozy looking patrol jumped into a vehicle and sped off to investigate the source of the noise. Ahead of us, Guardians and guard robots poured out of the dome, headed for the area of the explosion. I took out the polyscope and peered at the structure. Where the car had exploded, a large crack had formed which headed up the side for some considerable distance. Investigating that should keep them occupied for a while.

Our walk to the front door of the facility was now unimpeded by Guardians, robots or anything untoward. We tip-toed carefully through the checkpoint and found ourselves in a large open courtyard. There were dozens of buildings of various sizes scattered around at all the points of the compass. Where was the best place to start? A large building off to the left in the middle distance proclaimed itself to be the science block and, directly opposite that was the weapons bunker. Neither seemed suitable so we walked past them heading towards the central hub of the dome. Guardians were still running around all over the place but none noticed us through the camo drive field.

"Computer centre," whispered the professor, pointing to a large, airy looking building that was conveniently labelled as such.

"We can shut it all down from in there and no one will be hurt."

I nodded in reply and we crept over to the entrance. Once inside, the professor turned off the camo drive so as to conserve the power. There was no one about, presumably they were all deployed elsewhere within the structure due to our diversion. We walked stealthily down a long, white corridor with multiple doors leading off in all directions. There were several secure looking doors which we ignored but at the far end, was a large set of double doors which led into an enormous chamber. It was absolutely stuffed to the gunnels with computer banks, interfaces and other IT paraphernalia. Large cables snaked across the floor in a flagrant breach of Union health and safety protocols, so we picked our way cautiously over them. In the centre of the room, surrounded by a large space was a cube shaped terminal with a large glowing crystal on the top. Running through the centre of this was a strip of metal, about two centimetres wide which looked suspiciously like the material from Ventos. This flashed strange colours from time to time but mostly reflected the solid bluish hue from the crystal. Every so often, a spark would leap out from the middle of it and connect with one of the multiple lengths of cable which branched out in all directions. These led into the back of huge terminals and everything within the room hummed with an annoying buzz. The professor pointed at the cube and said:

"That looks like a control module of some sort."

"Yes." I agreed, trying to sound as if I knew what he meant.

"If we can sever its connection to the remainder of the computer terminals, the whole room should shut down and, if we can do enough damage, the whole operation would be crippled. It could take them weeks to recover." I nodded again.

As we approached the cube, the air became thick with a feeling of static electricity and sparks started to jump from us to the various assorted computer components. A particularly nasty spark hit me on the side of the face as we approached making me jump and exclaim in surprise. The professor stopped me from going any further by sticking his arm out in front of me. We were about two metres away.

"Too much electrostatic charge," he whispered. "We can't get too close or else we could end up electrocuted."

"Ok. How do we turn it off then?" I asked earnestly.

"Hmm. I don't quite know. Yet."

We stood there for a few seconds, pondering the problem. As we stood and watched the sparks leap from the centre out to the terminals, I realised there was a pattern - they ran anticlockwise around the room, to each of the eight main terminals in a sequence at twenty second intervals. Finally, he turned to me and said:

"Trojan. But I'll need to hack the system – it'll take me some time."

He walked over to one of the main terminals off to the left and brought up the 3D screen up in the air in front of him. Then he grabbed a handy chair, spun it so it was facing the right way and sat down.

Within seconds he was typing away happily at the keyboard, muttering to himself as he did so. After a few seconds, he looked up.

"I need to hack through four levels of firewalls and get to the main external operating system in order to create the Trojan outside the CPU so that I can insert it into the OS. This is probably going to take about an hour."

I looked at my chronometer.

"I hope you've got time before we get discovered!"

"Yeah, it'll be fine. Don't panic!" he said cheerfully and grinned at me.

"Are you sure?" I replied slowly, "Because I'm not!" and left him to get on with it.

He then returned to his typing and muttering so I wondered over to the door to keep an eye out. There was no one in the corridor but I had the sneaking suspicion that it was all a little too quiet. As I had nothing to do, I took the FPO out from the backpack. It was looking a little better now after a rest and was starting to act like its old self. It squeaked happily as I stroked the back of its body. I spoke to it quietly and it seemed to respond, answering my sentences with little squeaks and "pipping" noises which I'd never heard it make before. I wondered if it was trying to communicate with me somehow. I thought for a second and put it on the floor and let it gambol about happily, every so often it paused and looked at me as if to get approval. I looked at it and smiled. I'd never had a pet in my life before and so this was a welcome change. The little green thing was quite at home on Earth now, it seemed to have adjusted to the gravity during its captivity. It didn't seem to mind being lugged about in the backpack and as long as it was fed with UV light and fussed a bit, it seemed perfectly cheerful. I dug about in my coat pocket and found a small piece of reusable paper which I scrumpled into a small ball and threw it back into the room a metre or two. The FPO looked at me puzzled and then ran off towards it. Using its front prongs, it batted the impromptu ball back towards me and we had what could only be described as the world's first game of mini-football with an alien life form. It seemed really contented and bounded merrily about kicking the ball back to me with an unerring sense of accuracy.

We must have played for quite a while when the FPO suddenly stopped playing and squeaked loudly three times. It then cowered down and hid behind a computer bank.
"What's wrong?" I asked surreptitiously and then glanced out through the rectangular pane of glass. A squad of four Guardians were marching down the corridor, heading directly for us. All were armed and wore an expression of extreme annoyance. They also had with them two of the guard robots like the ones I had seen back on Ventos. I swiped the FPO up from the floor and as carefully as I could, placed it back into the backpack.
"Professor", I said urgently. "We've got company!"

"Bugger. The Union, again!" he murmured. "I need about another half an hour to finish this! I must've tripped an alarm!"

"Better hide and hope they go away then!" I replied sarcastically.

He thought for a second, shouted "Catch!" and threw me the portable camo drive parts. He ran across the room to a tangled mass of wires and large computer banks which were flashing with numerous coloured lights and ducked behind them. I ran in the opposite direction and hid behind a corresponding collection of computer consoles just in time as the squad entered the room.

"We know you're in here," shouted the lead Guardian. "You might as well surrender, there's no way out of this room. I've got five Guardians in the medical unit thanks to your prank with the exploding car and I am not in the mood to take any more shit from anyone!"

I remained still, as did the professor. A random spark shot across from the central cube and earthed itself just to my left but I kept my nerve.

"Stop trying to hide," he yelled, clearly getting even more annoyed. "I'm quite prepared to tear this room apart so you are only delaying the inevitable."

He then made one of those hand gestures which only military people seem to understand and the robots and the humans fanned out and began to search the room, methodically moving from one terminal to another and making plenty of noise while doing it – presumably to scare us both into giving away our positions. However, I remained still and, as far as I could tell, so did the professor.

As I sat crouched behind the computer bank, it occurred to me that if they caught me with the FPO, they would just continue their experiments on it and probably end up killing it even if they did capture the remainder of the population on Ventos. So I carefully removed the little creature from the backpack and placed it on the floor.

"Run!" I said to it quietly, butting its rear end with the palm of my hand. Luckily, the Guardians and robots were making so much noise that they failed to hear me. The little creature raised a prong questioningly at me and then scuttled underneath a nearby computer box, squeezing itself quite efficiently into the gap between the floor and the casing. The patrol was getting closer and closer all the time and it was only a matter of time before we were discovered. I peeped round the corner of the boxy terminal and was astonished to see that the professor had emerged from his hiding place and was walking out into the room with his hands up.

"Ok," he said quietly. "I give in."
The Guardians pounced on him and tied his hands behind his back.

"Take him to the cells!" yelled the patrol commander. The professor was led off out of the room by two Guardians, one holding onto each arm and disappeared from sight.

"I know there is still someone else here," he said once they had left.

I remained still and thought quickly about what I could do. He was right, there was no escape route. Then I remembered the professor had given me the portable camo drive so I fished the two components out of the backpack and brought them together. The nearest guardian to me looked over to where I was hidden for a split second just as I disappeared from view.

"I can see you," he said in a sing song voice. "Don't think your portable camo drive thing can hide you now!"

I remained silent and still while he waved his assault rifle around aimlessly all the while approaching my position. He clearly hadn't seen me and was trying to scare me into giving away my location.

"Come on out, I've not got all day," he continued.

I looked around in panic for a distraction or a weapon. Just on the computer bench in front of me was a large wrench. It was very solid looking so I stepped forward and grabbed it and quickly withdrew it into the distortion field. I waited until the Guardian was nearby and then threw it, fairly accurately, at his head. It connected with his helmet with a satisfying clang and he staggered over and fell down. By the time he was on his feet, I had run past him heading as fast as I could towards the door. I reached it at a dead run and shoved it open where I then proceeded to go head over heels as I tripped over a well concealed tripwire. The two halves of the camo drive split apart in mid-air and I became visible, sprawled on the floor, bruised and shaken while Tollie stood over me.

"Gotya, again!" he said grinning evilly. "To the cells with this one too!"

I was relieved of my backpack and the parts of the camo drive and then hauled to my feet and dragged off down the corridor. The Guardians did not speak to me as they heaved me out of the building and round the corner to what was presumably a prison block. Once inside, I was led down a long dark corridor with very poor lighting and then, after what seemed like a very long time, I was unceremoniously dumped into a cell. The cell itself was rather like the ones on the ship I'd been incarcerated in – they obviously had a job lot order of cells from the architect so once again, I found myself sitting on an uncomfortable bed looking at a clock on the wall. This one ticked in a really irritating way as if to remind me that I was stuck in here, all alone. The other main difference between this cell and the others I had occupied was a small electronic number pad which was sealed into the wall of the cell. I picked at the edge of it with my fingernails but it was impossible to lever off the front to get to the electronics and, even if I could, I wouldn't have the faintest idea of how to open the door. It was all completely hopeless so I sat on the bed and waited for something else bad to happen.

Despite the irritating clock, I let my mind drift and so I didn't know how long I sat there hugging my knees and humming Schubert to myself to keep my spirits up. My reverie was shattered when the panel in the bottom of the door opened and a very poor looking meal was thrust through. No one said anything through the intercom but I walked over and inspected it warily.

"Baked beans on toast?" I yelled ineffectively. "I'd rather eat a roasted wellington boot! And the desert has bloody raisins in it!" I added.

"This Tealog looks vile too and you've probably drugged it!" I yelled at the door and kicked the mug over onto the floor. It pooled slowly on the uneven floor, steaming gently.

Disgustedly, I pondered that maybe it was some sort of psychological torture as it was almost as if they knew what sort of foods I hated and served them intentionally. I shook my head sadly and returned to the so-called bed and sat, staring into space, humming. In due course, I felt sufficiently tired to lie down and try and sleep. I must have dozed off at some point because, when I awoke, the door was ajar and the professor was stood there shouting at me.

"Get up, we're getting out of here!" he said. I shook my head to try and dislodge the remnants of sleepiness from my brain. This worked tolerably well and I staggered over to him.

"What's happening?" I asked.

"I'm breaking you out. I managed to hack the door entry mechanism using the metal bracelet from my arm, it enabled me to short circuit the entry mechanism. C'mon, we've not got long before they discover we've got out!"

We ran along the dark corridor. At the far end was a Guardian station, guarded by two burly looking personnel. Neither of them seemed especially alert as they were busy looking at their 3D hologrammatic screen and pointing and laughing at whatever drivel they were watching. Luckily for us, it was so dark in the corridor that we remained almost invisible until we rushed at them. They didn't have time to draw their weapons before they were rendered unconscious with a few choice punches. Once outside, we hid beside a pile of pallets which was just outside the prison block. It must have been well after midnight as it was dark and there were few people around. Every so often, the sounds of owls in the woods drifted across on the light breeze.

"Now what?" I whispered.

"Back to the control room so I can finish my programme and get this place shut down."

"Excellent, let's trash this thing for once and for all!" I said heroically.

It was very cloudy so there was no moonlight so we were able to creep undetected across the courtyard between the buildings and soon we were close to the control room. At the front, it was guarded by six armed guards.

"Bugger!" said the professor dejectedly. "We could possibly surprise two of them but not six."

"Hmm. Is there a back way in?"

"No idea," he scratched his head thoughtfully, "Let's have a look."

We crept carefully around the perimeter of the building. Roughly half way around there was a vent which was presumably part of the heating or cooling system. It was about a metre and a half off the ground so was fairly easy to access. It took a few seconds for us to prise off the grill and place it quietly on the floor.

"You go in and I'll follow," he said.

I nodded and hefted myself up to the ledge. It was a long straight metal duct which, after a short while bifurcated and became narrower. There was no noise aside from a clunk every so often which I assumed was the professor behind me. I followed the left hand channel along and then after a sharp right turn, I found my way blocked by an enormous fan. It was metal and was almost the same size as the duct so there was no way of getting past it. I couldn't even fit my fingers around the edges without lacerating my hands so I awkwardly wriggled backwards and took the other fork instead. This one led to a small service area which was about two metres square and contained condensers and so on. Heading off from this was another tunnel, much narrower than the one I'd crawled down, which seemed to be heading in the right direction for the main room. It was a very tight squeeze but I crammed myself in, arms pointing forward into the space and edged along, using my hands and feet as leverage to push and pull myself along. I reached the end of the tunnel and there was another grill, much smaller than the other one we'd had to remove outside and I pushed at it with my hands, straining until it popped off and landed with a metallic clang on the floor on the other side. I held my breath and waited for a few seconds. There was no sound aside from the fizzing and sparking noises familiar from earlier on. I pushed myself forward a little further so the top half of my torso was sticking out of the vent.

"I'm here," came a quiet voice in the darkness. I heard footfalls and the professor grabbed my hands and pulled me out of the vent. I sat on the floor, exhausted and panting and then I asked him how he'd got in.

"I found another tunnel," he replied. "It led directly here. I've been working on the programme for twenty minutes and I've nearly finished it."

"Great," I replied. "Then we can get out of here?"

He strolled nonchalantly over to the control panel and pulled up the 3D head up display and continued to work. After several minutes, he closed down the display and turned to me and said:

"It's done. It'll take ten minutes for the system to reboot but I suggest we don't hang around. I've created a Trojan that will shut down all the cooling fans to the main control computer and that cube thing over there" - he pointed at it - "simultaneously so the whole thing will shut down as it gets overheated. It might even catch fire and explode too. It's always best to be sure."

"Why didn't you just nuke it from orbit 'just to be sure'?" I quipped in response.
He smirked at me and said:

"No plutonium unfortunately! Let's get out of here!"

We turned to the main doors. It would take too long to try to crawl along the vents so the only option was to surprise the guards on the way out and try to get clear of the area in time. We ran as quietly as possible along the main corridor but weirdly, there were no Guardians at the doorway when we got there.

"Where are they?" I asked.

"No idea, must've gone for a Tealog break or something?" he replied.

"Hmm..." I said thoughtfully.

I then had one of those horrible feelings that I'd forgotten something important and then I realised I'd left the FPO behind.

"Idiot!" I cursed to myself. I then looked at the professor and said "I need to go back for the FPO, it'll be somewhere in the main computer room. You should get out while you can."

"No, don't worry, I'll help you find it," he replied quickly.

We ran back into the building. By my estimation we had about eight minutes to find the FPO and get out before all hell broke loose.

I jogged as quickly as was safe around the main computer room to where I had left my small green friend. From time to time I made squeaking noises in an effort to attract it. We searched as best we could but couldn't find it anywhere. Time was running out. In desperation, I turned on the UV torch on my chronometer and shone it about into the darkest corners of the room. A small questioning squeak came as a response. I ran over and scooped up my little friend.

"Found it!" I shouted as loudly as I dared. The professor joined me within a few seconds.

"That's great news," he said. "But…" he said as he looked down at his chronometer, "we're right out of time – three Mississippi – two Mississippi – one Mississippi…the programme will now be rebooting, we ought to take cover, just in case." And with that, he ducked behind a computer bank. I joined him a few milliseconds later.

"This way," he said indicating a gap behind a large computer bank that would take us back in the general direction of the main doors. There was then a loud screeching noise as all the fans ceased to operate and the room began to get warm very quickly. We sprinted along behind the bank of computers that ran parallel to the wall of the room, heading towards the door but as we approached the doors, a group of heavily armed Guardians entered. At the head of them was Tollie looking as ugly as usual.

"You again!" we both said just as the system began to go critical and a nasty charring smell began to make it unpleasant to breathe.

"Run!" I yelled. The Guardians looked perplexed for a fraction of a minute, Tollie sniffed experimentally, correctly deduced that something bad was about to happen and we all ran.

We reached the main corridor at a flat out run just as it got too warm for humans to tolerate. As we proceeded along the main corridor, the smell of burning became extremely noxious as the overheated cables melted. We exited the building at high velocity and some of us tripped over into a pile in the mud in the open space outside the building. Behind us, there was an almighty fizzing sound and then silence. We all looked around puzzled for a second and then there was an enormous 'whoomph' sound and we were all knocked to the ground. I lay still for a few seconds and then carefully got to my feet. The Guardians were in various states of confusion and seemed to pose no threat, at least for now. Suddenly the FPO squeaked cheerily from the backpack bringing my attention back to the here and now. I looked around for the professor. He wasn't far away and was lying on the ground half submerged in a puddle. I staggered and stumbled my way over to him.

"Professor?" I asked anxiously, "Are you ok?" He groaned and opened his eyes and turned over.

"Did it work?" he asked weakly.

"Yes, I think so – it certainly looks like it!" I turned round and surveyed at the building. It was amazingly fundamentally intact although the doors were hanging off the hinges and the smell of burning insulation was quite obvious as it drifted through the shattered portal. I helped the professor to his feet, he seemed more like his normal self now but just a little shaken.

"We should check," he said smiling and looking slightly menacing.

"Ok!" I said and turned round and then I felt something hit me on the back of the head and I passed out.

I woke up in a comfy bed in a light and airy room. A nurse was fiddling with a 3D display on the opposite wall. My head hurt with a dull ache and when I felt my skull, my hair had been shaved off and I could feel the faint tell-tale traces of lumpy scar tissue over the crown of my skull.

"Nurse?" I asked weakly. "What happened?" She stood up and approached my bed. She was very pretty.

"Ah, Mister Heath, you are awake at last. You are in the medical unit at Bełchatów station. You had some shrapnel in your skull from falling debris. We had to operate to remove it." She had a faint Polish accent and her English was superb, far better than my Polish.

"Oh," I said. "Is the professor ok too?"

"Yes, he is fine," she replied smiling broadly. "He will come and see you soon. I will tell him you are awake. You should probably rest, you have been in a medically induced coma for some days while your brain swelling went down. I will get you some proper tea!" she said smiling even more broadly and then quickly left the room.

I lay back and looked out of the window. It was another fine and sunny day and everything looked serene and calm. On the right hand bedside table, there was a dirt box and, hiding in the bottom I could just make out the shape of the FPO. At least it was safe as well. On my left was an automatic drip which mechanically withdrew the needle from my arm when I moved into an upright sitting position to wait for my tea. Presently, the nurse returned and proffered me a mug. It was excellent and I relaxed back into the pillows and savoured the only proper cup of tea I had had in months.

"The professor will be with you shortly," she said and smiled happily as she left the room.

I didn't have long to wait and the professor walked confidently into the room. He looked somehow more imposing than before and he had a strange metal cap attached to his skull. He grabbed a chair from the corner of the room and settled down beside my bed.

"Are you ok now old chap?" he asked softly. "We thought we'd lost you for a while."

I nodded carefully and replied that I was feeling much better now.

"That's splendid news!" he exclaimed far too effusively.

I frowned and pointed to his head and asked, "What is that thing on your head?"

"It's a receiver of my own design," he said flatly. "It's based upon some of the things I got from the Mickleover Union site. It channels all of the computing power for controlling The Union into my brain so I can direct operations from here without need for a central nexus point."

My mouth fell open. He noticed this but continued in the same flat voice,

"Well, what did you expect? The destruction of the old guard of The Union would've left an enormous power vacuum, any old bunch of nutters could have taken over and plunged the world into chaos. I am a genius so it seemed fitting that I should take over and keep things on an even keel."

I said nothing and he continued:

"It's ok old friend. You can go back to your old job, all charges against you have been waived and you've been reinstated into a more senior position. Consider it a personal gift from me – after all, you've been extremely helpful in enabling me to take over." I opened my mouth to speak but again nothing came out.

"Don't worry, everything is under control and everything is going to be fine. I've not suddenly grown two noses or become a total twat, I'm still your friend!" he replied.

"But..." I finally managed to stammer. I stopped and thought for a second and then said:

"Well, I can see you've still got the one nose but I'm not entirely sure about the twat bit!"

The professor said nothing, scratched his ear and then said offhandedly:

"While you were unconscious, we did some neurological tests," he continued in a level tone of voice. "Turns out your brain chemistry and structure is subtly different to the many other people we've tested."

He paused momentarily before continuing, staring ahead.

"We think it might be because of your continued exposure to the minerals on Ventos. Really interestingly, it turns out that your main drive to 'do the right thing' is anger – it forces you to take potentially dangerous risks in order to try and set events on a path which you feel is the right one, no matter how foolhardy that might be. So, it would be worth your while doing exactly as we say as we've installed a little something in your brain which will prevent you from doing anything contrary to the interests of The Union. It's basically a modified mind control bracelet bridging a few circuits which we've implanted in your amygdala to make you less, shall we say… liable to get angry and rebel or try something heroic to make things fit with your perceived ideas of how things should be."

He paused for a while and steepled his fingers in front of his face.

"Now, you are awake and the medical staff have informed me that you are fit enough to go home. Your ship is parked outside and you can take your FPO with you and leave. Go back to your old life and let me get on with the business of controlling the planet. We now know there are aliens out there." At this point, he glanced sideways at the dirt box.

"So we need to be prepared for any possible invasions."

With that, he stood up, bowed his head slightly in my direction, waved goodbye and walked out of the room. I lay back on the comfy pillow, my mind whirling with numerous thoughts.

Chapter six – Return to Ventos

I was packed up and ready to go in less than an hour. For all his pontificating and grandstanding, the professor was true to his word. As I left the medical unit, Guardians stood back and let me pass, although some of them shot me a looks of displeasure as I walked towards *The Cowrie*. The ship's ramp extended and the last person to speak to me as I boarded, was Tollie. He cheerfully informed me with an evil grin, just as I was ascending the ramp, that the computer aided navigational system (CAM) autopilot had been set to return me to the landing strip where I had taken off all those months ago. He also told me that the navigational system was encrypted with an unbreakable cypher so there was no way I could prevent the ship from doing anything it hadn't been programmed to do. He also added sneerily that it was tied into the main power relay so messing with it would be stupid and probably fatal and that it was programmed with a low altitude flight so that I could be observed. His final parting words were "Have a safe flight!" delivered with his trademark sneering sarcasm. I had no choice but to go home and do as I was told.

Despite the implant, I did not feel any different aside from a sort of numbness whenever I thought about something which had previously made me angry. Aside from that, there was a low level humming sound which seemed to emanate from within the confines of my skull. It was maddening but overall I felt as though I should be angry, rather than actually being so. As I dejectedly flew over the former Polish border, it occurred to me that the FPOs on Ventos were going to be massacred sometime within the next few days. I did not feel unduly stressed or feel the need to do anything about it so whatever they had done to my brain was clearly working. My own FPO was still snuggled safely in its dirt box and seemed happy enough, not that I'd seen it since I had enticed it out from behind the computer banks in the compound. It was presumably recovering from the shock of its incarceration. However, to kill some time, I decided to try to get it to come out and play football with a piece of scrumpled up rewritable paper. I tried to encourage it by flicking the ball of paper from one hand to the other and making squeaking noises but it obviously didn't want to move. Puzzled, I stuck my hand into the dirt and tried to tickle it but even then, it didn't move at all. That was weird, usually it was only too keen to come out and play. I dug down into the dirt. The FPO did not respond so I lifted it out from the debris and brushed the dirt off. Instead of the reddish / greenish coloured friendly little creature that squeaked happily when it saw me, there was a rubbery and clearly artificial, toy. The bastards. They'd lied to me, my FPO was still in Poland and would be killed along with the rest of them. Despite my feelings, I felt powerless and I slunk miserably back in the pilots chair and consoled myself with a very big mug of

Tealog. I felt weary, tired and slightly sick but there was nothing more that I could do.

The ship flew on. Gloomily, I noticed that with each moment, it was growing darker echoing my mood. This was really weird, it was the middle of the day and so should be broad daylight. Puzzled, I checked my portable chronometer, it was mid-afternoon. I checked the chronometer again, the inbuilt weather app cheerfully informed me there was a huge, level twelve storm brewing over the English Channel, directly in my flight path. There are twelve levels of storm types, defined by the strength of the wind and the power contained in the lightning. Level twelve was generally regarded as "If you wish to be suicidal, try flying in that. Lightning strikes can pierce almost any outer hull of a ship, no matter how well protected and insulated". Only a total nutcase would attempt any kind of suborbital flight in this sort of weather so the rest of the flight was going to be interesting, especially as the course was programmed in and impossible to override.

"Shit!" I said aloud with as much feeling as was possible with an inhibitor chip in my brain.

A few seconds later, the first really powerful blast of wind hit the ship and shoved it sideways. The autopilot control struggled to bring the ship back to the correct heading by firing the manoeuvring thrusters. The green 'ok' light lit up for a few seconds before going off again as the ship veered off in the opposite direction. The wind shear must have been incredible as time and again the autopilot struggled to control the ship. I was making very little headway with the weather seeming to try and force me to change course at every opportunity and, just as I thought things couldn't get any worse, the lightning started. A huge forked prong smashed into the ship, punched a hole in the outer skin of the fuselage on the port side just behind the cockpit and, within seconds all the electrical systems were dead. At least the autopilot was destroyed now, I thought just before a second lightning strike hit the wing on the starboard side of the ship and sent us into a shallow downward spiral.

"Shit! Shit! Shit!" I yelled as the ship began to plunge down towards the sea. It was impossible to tell where I was but crashing into the sea or land would mean almost certain death especially as the outer skin of the ship was compromised. Luckily, as we were at low altitude, the change in air pressure was not catastrophic or else I might have been sucked out of the ship. I stood up in panic, uncertain of what to do next.

As I looked around the interior of my cockpit, panicking and struggling to stay on my feet, a gust of wind blew a squall of rain in through the hole and with it, a ball of lightning. It crackled as it floated about the airspace, calmly bouncing off things as it went. It hissed as the droplets of rainwater boiled as they came into contact with it. I watched it for half a second in fascination and then spun round and sat back at the controls. It was remotely possible that I might be able to glide the ship in, if I could just get out of the spin. I remembered my combat training from the ice chamber on Ventos and pulled the manual control joystick as hard as I could towards me, turning it in the direction of the spin in a vain attempt to level off and then fired the port side jets. At least this way, the main flaps and ailerons might be able to give me some control in my descent. It seemed to be starting to work when I became aware of a hissing and burning smell just behind my left ear. I turned round just as the ball lightning engulfed my cranium and I felt a searing pain all over my head. I yelled and passed out.

     I awoke. Comparing the pain in my head to the headache that I had when I awoke from my coma, would be like comparing a pea to the size of the Earth. The sensation was so intense that I nearly passed out again immediately. My right leg also seemed in a bad way and there was quite a lot of blood around. I peered myopically out of the front view screen, trying not to scream with the pain in my head. The view was a flat, featureless green field with the occasional bramble and small trees scattered randomly about. I pushed down on the arms of the chair and tried to stagger to my feet but didn't get very far. To make it worse, I threw up due to the agony and sagged back into the chair. When I opened my eyes again, my head felt slightly better than before but the pain in my leg was awful. It must be fractured, I thought as I used my good leg to lever myself to a standing position. I hopped excruciatingly and slowly towards the stern of the ship where the first aid kit was, supporting myself on whatever I could. It took me ages but I eventually found the first aid kit, broken open in the corner. Luckily nothing medicinal was damaged so I slumped painfully down on the floor and gave myself a massive injection of painkillers. Once I had done this, I looked at my leg. This was obviously badly broken as the bone was slightly sticking out through my trousers. Not far away were the emergency callipers so I attached them to the muscles either side of the break and set them to straighten the damaged limb. Even though I had braced myself and taken painkillers, the intense stab of agony was intolerable and I almost passed out again as the bones snapped back into place. Once this was done, I wrapped a goodly length of bandage around it and hoped for the best.

While I administered medicines and several metres of temposkin, it dawned on me that I seemed to no longer have the buzzing sound from within my skull. At first, I thought I might have been mistaken but, as the pain from my assorted injuries began to recede, I realised there was no sound. It struck me as odd because there was clearly no way of removing the chip without help from a very skilled brain surgeon. As I peered into the mirror in the first aid kit box, I realised that the ball lightning must have shorted it out when it had connected with my head. Although the painkillers and other pains had covered it, my face and head were quite badly burned and I would need to locate an emergency burns mask to repair that damage. The lightening would also explain the damage to the ship – it had been attracted to the areas of highest potential difference so must have taken out the main relay in the wall, just behind the cockpit and also destroyed the chip in my brain. Well, at least that was one positive from all of this. The other thing keeping me going was that I was absolutely furious, angrier than I had ever been in my entire life. I had numerous injuries, no hair, the professor had betrayed me for his own twisted ends and had sent me off to die and they were going to kill my FPO and all of the other ones as well. One way or another, I was going to make them pay dearly for this.

    I found the burns mask close to the first aid kit and placed it over my face. Ok, I now looked like something from an old horror film as well. I'd have to wear it for a few days but the gentle massaging combined with the dermal regeneration fields and hydrating fluids would at least mean that I would not be scarred badly. However, it would probably mean I would never be able to grow a beard or have any hair on my head ever again. I clamped the thing in place and waited for the initial sense of intense claustrophobia to diminish. However, I would need to leave the accursed thing in place to repair the burns and general damage to my head.

I stumbled awkwardly across the ship to the airlock and deployed the ramp. Luckily, this worked fine and I was able to walk slowly and stiffly out of the wreck of *The Cowrie*. The emergency crash landing mechanisms had all fired simultaneously as I'd impacted the ground and there was expanded foamy material all over the place, covering the floor of the small crater the ship had excavated. Despite this system working perfectly, the ship was in rough shape, the outer shell of the hull was badly scorched in many places and there was a twenty by forty centimetres hole where the first lighting strike had taken out the main power relay. The left wing was also bent and had a large void in it. As far as I could tell visually, the engines seemed fine and so I should be able to take off and fly, once I had done sufficient emergency maintenance. The same kit I had used to make running repairs while in the pocket of the future universe would easily fix a lot of the smaller holes but the big one was going to be a problem. Luckily, I had a reserve power relay which, with the help of several metres of superconducting filament enabled me, with the aid of more painkillers and within a couple of hours, to restore power to the main controls.

Once this was done, it was easier to assess the extent of the damage. It was not good - there were dozens and dozens of little red indicators on the control panel, each corresponding to some system that was damaged or not working at full capacity. Scanning the outer skin also pointed out the numerous holes in the fuselage, many of which I had not noted before. I would now have to methodically go around and seal them, one by one. I sat back in the chair and administered several more oral and injected doses of painkillers. I also injected some more osteocytes to assist with the broken leg. I would hopefully now be able to work without passing out from the pain.

The furious, all consuming anger and need for revenge made me force myself to continue with the repairs. I had to save the FPOs and I was not going to let the bastard Union get away with anything more. Once the inside of the ship was a little more ordered, I decided to have a look outside and fix some of the larger damage so I extended the ramp and limped painfully down it. Although I had no idea where I was, there seemed to be no one about so at least for now, I was undisturbed.

Outside the ship, I ascertained the broken wing was luckily close to the ground and with some painful manoeuvring, I was able to sit on the follower and work on welding and replacing the damaged parts using some of the metal sheets I'd stolen from The Union ship on Ventos. I stomped as furiously as I could in and out of the ship numerous times and each time I initialised the power to the main console, fewer and fewer of the lights were lit. By the time I collapsed exhausted into bed many hours later, maybe half of them that had shown as a problem originally, had become green. Despite my all-consuming anger, I somehow managed to sleep due to the painkillers and the usual sleeping tablets.

The next day dawned grey and dull. While I waited for the latest batch of painkillers to kick in, it occurred to me that I had no idea where I was. At the main console, I pulled up the topographic scans of the area. I had crashed in the middle of a flat area and behind me, facing away from the prow of the ship and over a cliff were a series of short white limestone pointed structures that led off into the sea. At the end, partly submerged in the water, were the remnants of a red and white striped lighthouse. This was a give-away as to where I was – I had crash landed on the peninsula just inland on the now uninhabited Isle of Wight, just near the Needles. Luckily I had landed on the land part and not half way over a cliff or, worse still, on the beach as I would most likely have drowned as the ship filled with water as the tide came in. I also pondered why no one had come to find me but the only explanation that I could think of was the Union were too busy being reorganised by the double-crossing professor to worry about me. Either that, or they assumed that I had been killed in the storm or the crash.

My main job was fixing the ragged hole in the hull where the power relay had been vaporised. I tied a few strands of filament over the inside of the hole and gradually patched across, building up the layers so I had a somewhat flimsy and flexible outer skin. Then I welded a chunk of metal to the inside of this and fixed the edges down with the putty-like repair material used to fill the gaps around the edges. Hopefully, it would be air tight once I was in space. I then plugged the five centimetres thick gap between the inner and outer hulls with the standard insulation, shoved the relay back in roughly the right place and then spot welded another plate of metal over the top, sealing it from the inside. By the conclusion of the second day, almost all of the lights were green and the remaining damaged systems could be repaired *en route* to Ventos where hopefully I could intercept the ship before it harvested the FPOs. My rage and thirst for revenge at the whole situation had not abated but I had managed to channel it into repairing the ship. The pain from my leg had all but subsided as the osteocyte injections helped to repair the damage and the painkillers kept my other injuries from incapacitating me.

By the third day, which dawned brightly with sunshine emanating weakly from behind some small white cumulonimbus clouds, I felt far better. My leg felt almost ok as the assorted drugs and injections of osteocytes continued their magic, knitting together the damaged bones. Most of the smaller injuries had healed thanks to the temposkin and my head felt almost normal. I wasn't exactly firing on all cylinders but I was, at least, functioning mostly acceptably. The drugs I took to sleep seemed to be working well too as I had been sleeping extremely deeply, obviously aiding my recovery.

Once I got myself going, I continued with my toils. As the lightning strike had destroyed the control box for my pre-programmed flight home, I needed to rebuild and reconfigure the entire autopilot system. This meant fortunately that no trace of The Union's programmed course was left. I had made recent repairs to the relays for the solar cells so once it warmed up and the sun came out, the ship was charging up correctly. Weapons were not yet operational as the power surge from the lightning had shorted them out completely but I had the necessary spares and time to fix those as I made my way to Ventos. I also added the new power core I'd stolen from The Union and, after a few tests, I determined that the ship was ready.

By now it was early afternoon, so I had some food and made final preparations to leave. I sat in the pilot's chair and test fired the suborbital engines. They started up immediately and the ship lifted clear of the debris field. She wobbled a bit as she broke free of the crash landing foam. It occurred to me that if I crashed again, I would be in trouble as I would have no protection from the force of any impact. The foam would have to be replenished at some point in the future when I had the time and facilities to do it but for now, it would have to wait. I landed the ship a few metres away from the crater and ran some more final checks, including the structural integrity by increasing the pressure within the ship so that any leaks would show. Everything registered as air tight. Lastly, in an act of defiance, I threw the replica FPO out through the airlock so I would not be reminded of my gullibility.

By my estimations, The Union ship would take about three weeks to get to Ventos. They did have a head start but my ship, with the modifications was smaller and faster and, when they got to the planet, they would still need to locate the creatures. Seeing as the planet had been covered in a blanket of ice last time I'd seen it, this could potentially take them a while and would hopefully give me time to catch up. Despite this, I had no time to loose. I breathed in and set the new autopilot system with the fastest possible direct course for Ventos at maximum speed. I held my breath and crossed my fingers, activated the camo drive and fired the main thrusters. Within seconds, I was high in the atmosphere and headed out of Earth's orbit. Once clear of the Earth, I busied myself with the last few minor repairs and general tidying up. The FPOs dirt box was the last thing I dealt with. It was in about a million fragments, scattered around the place and tidying up that particular mess took me a long time.

At least now the ship was fully operational and the inside was habitable again. During the first part of the flight, I had briefly toyed with the idea of returning to Poland to rescue my FPO however, it occurred to me that they would most likely take it back to Ventos so they could process them all together. I kept thinking if only I could get to the planet in time to stop the cull. Thoughts like this made me even more impatient to get to my destination but there was no sign of any Union ships on sensors as *The Cowrie* sped through the area which had once been the Bok globule – now just a normal region of space with no sign of giant electric space-going jellyfish or dead versions of the planet Earth. Once I was within a day's flight of my destination, medical scans informed me that it was safe to remove my burns mask. Once I'd done this, I inspected the damage to my face and skull in the mirror in the bathroom. Ok, I wasn't quite as photogenic as I had been but at least I looked human. I also removed the leg brace as the medical scanners happily informed me that my leg was fully healed too.

From a tactical point of view, I plotted a course to fly round to the dark side of the planet, well away from any likelihood of detection. Presently, Ventos hoved into view on the main screen and, parked in a low orbit, was The Union ship. They appeared to be doing nothing, there was no traffic between the ship and the surface so it was possible they were scanning the planet for signs of the FPOs. Presumably, once they had located the area they were in, they would land and begin to collect them and then fly them back to Earth for processing.

I watched them from the safety of a higher orbit, further around the planet with the camo drive activated. Nothing happened for what seemed like an age and then, just as my impatience and anger seemed about to get the better of me and force me to make a rash decision, I noticed two small patrol ships launch from the ship. They flew down to the surface but I lost track of them due to the disturbed atmosphere. I thought for a second and then set a course to follow them. They clearly hadn't seen the need to use their camo drives as they were most likely not expecting company.

The planet was still frozen although the snow and ice were now showing signs of beginning to melt. Slushy lakes were located in what were presumably the craters that had pock marked the surface and the atmosphere, once cloudy with debris from the meteors, had become clearer so the sunlight was actually reaching the ground. Air temperatures were about 5°C uniformly across the whole of the planet so it was like a chilly English early winter day – nothing like it had been on my previous visit and far easier to get about in.

Scanning from the lower atmosphere revealed that the ground in the area they landed in was bumpy with ridges and furrows and covered with a mostly thin layer of snow. I flew in at a low angle so that the ship was obscured by the surface topography and the clouds, landing a few hundred metres away from the scout ships. The scanners showed six occupants who were milling about chipping at the ice and snow and they appeared to be talking earnestly to one another. They appeared to be moving slightly stiffly and mechanically and there was clearly something not quite right about them. I squirreled that observation away for later consideration.

At this range, there was no way I could determine what was being said but they were all carrying hand held scanners and radios and, after an initial conference, they spread out radially from a central point. I grabbed my backpack, exited the ship and stealthily made my way towards them. I stopped about a hundred metres away and hid behind a large snow covered rock, retrieved from the polyscope from my backpack and watched them carefully for some time. One of them suddenly shouted something and the others ran over to meet him. He then knelt down in the snow and pointed down into it. The others produced spades and small portable lasers from their backpacks and began to hack away at the ice. Within minutes, they had uncovered some sort of chamber as, even from where I was, I could see that a large hole had opened up and they were peering into the dark recesses below. One of them produced a harpoon like device and fired it into a nearby rock. He then attached a line to the pin and trailed it downwards into the depths below, attached what must have been a carabina to it and disappeared into the hole. A few minutes later, two other members of the group followed him down into the subterranean ice cavern. The three people left on the surface stood about looking cold and occasionally jumping about to keep warm. Then one of them grabbed his radio and put it to his ear. It was impossible to hear what was being said but he was clearly very concerned as he directed the other two to go down into the ice hole immediately. They did so reluctantly and then, finally, he too headed down.

Once they had all descended into the hole, I left my hiding place and sneaked closer to the entrance, hiding behind rocks at regular intervals. As I drew closer, I could hear terrified screams, yells and laser firing sounds from beneath and, every so often through the pool of light, I caught sight of something running quickly underneath. It didn't look like the green FPOs, the shape and configuration looked different. It dawned to me that they had found a nest of the carnivorous versions of my little friend and were now paying the price. I waited to see what would happen. After a few moments, the screaming ended and so I shone a torch down into the hole. I could clearly see that there was quite a lot of blood below me in the gloom and, more scarily, gleaming in the darkness, a fleshless skull grinned back at me. I walked silently over to the rock with the pin which they had secured the rope to and blasted it free so that it slithered into the hole. They may have been bad but they didn't deserve that fate. I thought for a moment and realised that it showed that the FPOs could survive under the ice. Therefore, there was a reasonable chance that my little friends' brethren had done the same somewhere else.

I ran a topographic scan of the area, comparing it to scans of the landscape before the ice. It revealed that I was stood near the top of part of the mountain range that had made me ill when I had attempted to cross last time and so, logically, orientating myself using the suns, the ocean was behind me and the town where I had made my home and the desert was ahead of me. That seemed to be the environment that the friendly FPOs favoured so I returned to my ship and took off. I realised that the interference from the weather would prevent The Union ship in orbit from detecting them so before I left, I flew over the hole in the ice where the people had died and blasted it shut with a few well aimed laser blasts. At least the dead Union employees would have a semi decent burial below ground.

Using my data from my previous flight, I was able to approximately pinpoint the location where the FPOs should be found. I reactivated the camo drive so that the Union didn't follow me to the FPOs hideout and landed in a flat area of snow which seemed to go on forever in all directions. A quick scan had revealed a small heat spot not far below the surface about five hundred metres away – I had seen that the FPOs could generate heat when needed and so it was likely that they were somewhere beneath my feet, surviving the winter cocooned together, a bit like penguins on Earth. I walked cautiously over to the area and, conscious of the fate of the six individuals I had observed, I carefully melted a ten centimetre hole in the ice, too small for me to climb through and hopefully also too small for anything vicious to climb out and get me. Once this was done, I lowered the polyscope into the void on a small length of superconducting filament and connected it remotely to my chronometer. At first, it was hard to spot anything at all on the screen but gradually my eyes adapted to the gloom and I could make out hundreds of greenish FPOs, packed like sardines into a rounded chamber about five metres in circumference. I needed to rescue them all or find some way of preventing The Union from getting to them. Obviously, I also needed to save my friend from the ship (assuming it was still on there) but, if I could secure this colony somewhere safe, then I could sort the other problem later on. I assume they wouldn't kill it until they had the whole payload that they needed as one on its own would be useless. It was highly likely there were more concentrations of the little green creatures elsewhere on the planet but for the time being, this one would have to be sufficient. Hopefully, The Union wouldn't go ahead without the whole payload.

I returned to the ship just as the weather took a turn for the worse. The snow started up again, the winds began to pick up and the temperature plunged. This would have the fortunate side effect of further distorting the energy signature from the ship to anyone who was scanning for it. I flew in closer to the area where the FPOs were hiding – landing right on top of it and obscuring the little hole I had made with the bulk of my ship, just in case. I sat for a moment considering my next move. Somehow I had to get all these FPOs somewhere safe. After a minute or two it dawned on me that this was an ex-mining ship and therefore was equipped with mining lasers and cutting equipment. If I could cut out the chamber, I could carry it somewhere else and hide it then all I would need to do was find a suitably defendable position. I had a brainwave – if I could find the old dome that The Union had installed near the metal spike, I could stay in there as it would be the last thing they'd expect.

I scanned the ice in order to determine the size of the chamber, set the lasers to cut deeply into the ice and melted out a broad circle, around seven metres in diameter so that there was plenty of space on either side of the hibernating creatures and their lair. Then I programmed the carrying straps to go down the channel I'd excavated and join up to meet in the middle – similar to what I had done in the ice cavern with the geothermal energy supply. Once these had all locked in place and created a mesh, all I needed to do was fly the chunk of ice to the dome. The whole operation had taken about an hour and I was aware that the ship in orbit could discover me at any point. My other concern was the weight of the ice, however the augmented ship should be more than capable of carrying the mass. All I needed to do next was locate the old dome. I compared the cartographic scans and the topographic ones from my previous visit and quickly ascertained that I was two hundred kilometres from the dome, if I flew in a straight line. It was an easy flight but the likelihood of discovery was growing greater by the minute and, with the engines running at full power, it was even more likely to be found. Driving across the ice would be impossible due to the payload and I would also be more vulnerable to attack from the air. I had no choice but to risk the short flight with the camo drive activated. I programmed in the course and set the engines for maximum suborbital burn. At that speed, I would be there in a matter in minutes and, with the unpleasant weather, I was at a lower risk of being detected so that was a help.

I fired the suborbital engines but restricted the height of the ship to ten metres above ground level. The swirling snow and the atmospheric distortion should cover my tracks, especially as I was flying over highly reflective snow and ice with rock underneath it. Maybe even the metallic debris would help to deflect some of the scans as well. I flew on for a few minutes in fairly atrocious weather. The winds were increasing in strength and the ship, with the additional weight of a huge block of ice slung underneath it, was pitching from side to side violently. The landscape ahead became increasingly rugged and there was less snow cover so I increased speed slightly to reduce the amount of time that I spent flying over that type of ground. In due course, I was flying down the seaward edge of the mountain range and heading along the beach towards the site of the dome. I could also see that the water of the ocean was no longer solid and was steaming slightly as the ice had all but dissipated as the weather improved.

The more I thought about it, one thing was troubling me - how I would get the FPOs into the dome? I gave up in the end and decided that it was a case of crossing that bridge when I got to it. My assumption was that the crack caused by the avalanche would not have been repaired fully so I would be able to fly in through that and carefully deposit the cargo of ice and FPOs. My hypothesis, when the dome appeared glinting on the horizon, appeared to be correct. Much of the dome was obscured by snow and drifts however there was still a large crack facing the seaward side of the mountains, as I had remembered it. I flew to the apex of the dome and carefully lowered the chunk of ice in through the fissure and then disconnected the straps. The ice sat there on the floor of the compound between two of the main buildings, towards the back of the dome. I then flew down to the main entrance and found a convenient overhang under the nearby cliffs in which to park the ship so it was not immediately visible from the air.

I grabbed my backpack and shoved as many provisions as was possible into the follower I'd stolen from The Union ship, descended the ramp and jogged quickly the last few metres into the dome. Once I passed through the mangled and abandoned main entrance, I looked carefully around. It looked as if the place was deserted - people had obviously left in a hurry as there was plenty of churned up mud on the ground and things were in disarray.

Cautiously, I continued to explore but I didn't get very far. Just as I was heading for the main control centre to see if I could get main power back up and running, I felt a gun pressed into the small of my back. A female voice hissed into my left ear:

"Put your hands where I can see them and turn around very slowly."

I did as I was told and found myself face to face with a tall, slim blonde woman in her mid-twenties dressed in Union clothes and looking scared witless.

"Who are you?" she asked breathlessly. "And what the hell happened to your face?"

"I'm Paul Heath," I replied.

She waved the gun menacingly in my direction just as several other people emerged from behind the nearby buildings.

"Prove it. We heard that you were dead!" she said.

"Nope, very much alive," I said lightly and added, "reports of my death have been greatly exaggerated!" I ignored her second question.

She gave me a look which implied that she thought I was a smartarse.

"Look," I sighed wearily, "if I roll up my sleeve you can take a DNA sample and run it through your identity checker, that'll verify I'm telling the truth."

"Ok," she said thoughtfully and another similarly dressed Union person passed her the necessary equipment. The blood sample was taken and within a couple of minutes, they both returned nodding wildly.

"Yes, he is Paul Franz Heath," he said excitedly, "although he looks like he's been in the wars a bit."

"Well," I bragged, "I've survived a major crash in my ship and all sorts of dangerous situations so I'm a bit battered and bruised. What's going on?"

"We were left behind when The Union evacuated the dome after you sabotaged the mining operation. They left us for dead." He paused and continued with barely concealed anger.

"We were the stragglers who couldn't get to the ships fast enough. None of us is military, we've got eleven people in all – a few engineers, a doctor, a mortician, several scientists and a personal assistant. None of us were coerced into wearing their jewellery as we actually wanted to explore this planet. Jodie over there (he pointed to the woman who'd initially held me at gunpoint) realised they were acting weirdly and it had something to do with the bracelets and bangles. We've survived here on rations for the last few months, in the hope of rescue but no one's come for us. Suffice to say, we are not the biggest fans of The Union since they left us here to freeze to death." He stopped speaking for a minute and looked wistful.

"We've lost a few along the way too, all because of The Union. We've been monitoring their broadcasts and heard that there has been a change of leadership and a professor from Cambridge is now in charge. I'm thinking that was your doing?" he said and waved the gun ineffectively at me.

"Yes, sorry about that, I screwed up," I said. "I was meaning to destroy the whole operation but he tricked me and used the situation to his advantage to get control. He's now in charge and uses his brain as a central console to control all of the computers via some sort of neural link he found before we destroyed the R and D dome near Derby."

Several of the group looked shocked and chorused that they hadn't been aware of that. I then gave them a brief overview of my trip to Poland with the professor and then a short history of my time on the Isle of Wight and the repairs I had had to make to *The Cowrie*.

After a few minutes, a strapping looking bloke who clearly spent time in a gym asked me why I'd airlifted a huge chunk of ice into the dome.

"It's the FPOs," I replied.

Everyone looked blank.

"Sorry, I should explain, I mean the little green creatures that run about and play in the dirt? You must have seen them. I call them FPOs, standing for Four Pronged Organism as they've got four legs."

Several of the group nodded and mumbled that they understood what I meant. I continued:

"The Union is planning to harvest them for their chloroplasts and use them as a fuel source on Earth. They wanted to exterminate the species but I have one as a pet and it was my only companion here on this planet for months so I've grown rather attached to it. I can't let them do that!"

"Where is it now?" asked the slim blonde woman.

"Oh, it's on the Union ship that's currently parked in orbit. That's come here to harvest them. They tried to find some earlier on but they got it wrong and found the less friendly relatives of the benign green ones. I'll just say they met a sticky end. We should get those I've rescued in the ice block somewhere safe, and quickly."

"We have freezers," piped up another man from the back of the group. "They could go in there. We can set the temperature to mimic the conditions in their hibernation chamber and they should be fine."

"Ok," I said. "Is that easy enough? How is the power grid here? Was it damaged by the avalanche?"

"The power grid's intact and working at one hundred and twenty percent output just to maintain the structural integrity of the dome with the crack in it. To be honest, we don't know how long it will last as it's under massive strain. The geothermal power isn't so much the problem, it's the distribution network which is creaking at the seams," he replied by way of an explanation.

"Right. In that case," said the muscular looking bloke, "we should repair the dome first. We would've done so before but we don't have any ships left as they took them all. We can use your ship, then we can get this place heated up properly and get everything working again and hold them off."

I thought about this for a few seconds.

"No," I said thoughtfully. "If we repair the dome, it'll be a dead giveaway that you have a ship. We need them to think you're helpless down here and they definitely shouldn't know that I'm here. They've already sentenced me to death."

I paused for effect and noted a series of audible gasps from my audience and then, shortly afterwards, murmurs of dissent amongst the group. Nonetheless, I continued:

"Having said that, I need to get onto the Union ship and rescue my pet. Now that there is a ship is in orbit, you could send a distress call and they may answer it. If they do, would there be a way to get on board undetected?"

A small pretty young woman stepped forward. I gawped at her for a second.

"Broken any glassware recently?" I asked, slightly nervously.

"What?" she said, looking bemused and slightly irritated.

"Last time I saw you, you dropped a volumetric flask in the lab."

"Oh, right, erm…yes I have been known to do that, perils of working in a lab," she said bashfully. "Anyway, the answer is no, I haven't." She paused and looked me full in the face.

"Your face is looking a little battered," she said. "We have a medical person here and a proper medical grade burns mask that would tidy up the damage and make you look like you did before. You'd need to wear it for three or four days but it would be better than the first aid kit version that you used to do that!" she said, waving her hand dismissively in my direction.

I felt somewhat aggrieved by this. As far as I was concerned I looked ok and not too dissimilar to before. I shrugged.

"But how does that help me to get on-board the ship and rescue the FPO?"
She looked at the floor for a second and then brightened up.

"We could put you in a wheelchair with your face obscured while the damage was healing properly, they'd never know it was you."

"That's a bit obvious," I responded flippantly. "They'd probably run some sort of DNA analysis to determine who the patient was and then I'd be captured. Anyone got any other ideas?"

I looked across the motley group. Another cadaverous looking chap who was stood towards the back held his hand up like a schoolchild wanting to answer a question in class and spoke up:

"We could put you in a coffin?" he said thoughtfully in a marked northern European accent.

"You what?" I replied incredulously.

"We could put you in a coffin," he repeated. "With the dermal regeneration kit over your face. It's standard procedure when a body is badly damaged that the face is restored to present it to loved ones so they can identify the body or, if they wanted an open casket funeral then at least it's not dissimilar to how the person looked in life. As Carlos said to you earlier, we've lost a few along the way. For example, Jones was swept away in a small second avalanche last week. We never found his body and he was about your size and stature. When The Union turn up to rescue us, we can bring you on-board in a coffin and you can let yourself out later on and find your pet."

"Ok," I said slowly "but what about my life signs?"

"We'd give you a suppressant and hide a vial of chemicals in the coffin to make you smell a bit off," said the tall blond woman. "They'd never suspect anything. We could also include some of the things Jones liked and so when they scanned the coffin, they'd find a dead body with the face obscured along with all his things. They wouldn't ask any questions, I'm sure."

"I need to think about this," I said. "But we won't have long, I suspect The Union will be preparing to launch more scout ships to try and find the FPOs. We need to hide these ones first."

Firstly we set about opening up the FPOs' hibernation chamber. Jodie, the tall blonde woman proved to be rather useful with laser weaponry and Elouisa, the laboratory analyst, was good at setting the electronics up on the freezers. It wasn't long before everything was ready. All we had to do was figure out how to wake the FPOs up and lead them into the chamber. It dawned on me that they were sightless but seemed to respond to smells so I ran back to the ship and returned with the smashed up remnants of the first dirt box I'd kept the FPO in. Once I explained what I had planned, we scatted the fragments in a trail from a newly melted hole in the edge of the block of ice to the door to the freezers, set them to automatically close and then waited for the temperature of the ice to rise sufficiently for them to revive from their state of torpor. We didn't have to wait long and soon the little green things were meandering, rather groggily one by one, into the freezer. Once all five hundred and thirty two of them were inside, we shut the door. Elouisa monitored them carefully to establish they were safely re-entering their hibernation and once their life signs showed that they were dropping off to sleep, she sent the distress call to the ship in orbit. Hopefully she'd managed to sound sufficiently pleading and this part of The Union would be a little more compassionate toward their fellow employees than the division which had abandoned them in the first place. We returned to *The Cowrie* and, on the way discussed the other steps in the plan which basically involved the others insinuating themselves in with the crew on board the ship. We grabbed anything which might be useful from my ship and then I activated the camo drive. Lastly, when we were safely clear, Jodie, using a laser rifle, skilfully brought down a load of ice and snow from the top of the cliff where I had parked, burying *The Cowrie* for the time being. While she did this, I changed into a spare Union uniform and then was introduced to my temporary home, had the surgical dermal regeneration mask fitted and was injected with the suppressant. I was unconscious within a few moments. The last thing I remembered was being told that the drugs would wear off in eight to ten hours.

***

Elouisa told me much, much later over a glass of wine that, not long afterwards, a scout ship had landed on the ruined landing strip at the front of the dome.

After a long discussion, they accepted everything they were told as gospel and let everyone on board, initially quarantining them from the remainder of the crew but once they docked with the large ship in orbit, they were allowed to mix freely. My coffin had been transported down to the bowels of the ship, in a refrigerated area near a storage bay. They had opened the coffin and briefly scrutinised my disguised features within but had left it at that. The presence of Jones's teddy bear, an unpleasant smell of decaying flesh and his collection of small but interesting rocks he'd found on the planet were sufficient to convince them the battered body inside was his.

***

     I woke up. Unsurprisingly, it was pitch black and rather cramped. The plastic inside of the coffin felt cold and uncomfortable and my face hurt as the mask did its job of reconfiguring the dermis and the epidermis on my skull, hopefully in a better way than had been done before. I lay there for a few minutes, waiting for the fogginess in my head to clear. I'd been told to expect this but what I really needed right now was a cup of Tealog or better still, proper tea. However, that would have to wait. I lay there in the dark for a few moments until I felt I was ready and then flicked on the light from my chronometer. Once the initial stab of pain in my eyes had subsided, I had a look around for the catch mechanism. When I found it, I fished the small knife I had secreted away from the cuff of the uniform. As the mortuary assistant Dave had explained, the best way to break the locking mechanism was to shove it straight into the keyhole. I stabbed at it hard and there was a loud click as I twisted the knife. I then slowly opened up the coffin and looked around. Once I determined the coast was clear, I carefully climbed out, like some corpse from an ancient horror film. There was no sound from the hinges and once clear of the coffin, I found myself in a deserted space measuring about ten metres squared. There were two other coffins, presumably occupied with less vital inhabitants. Feeling slightly squeamish, I crept past them, giving them a wide berth. It was freezing cold so I made my way quickly and as quietly as possible to the door. There were long clear bioplastic strips hanging down from the top of the door frame and I pushed these silently aside and peered into the room next door. It was too dark to see but there was no sound so I concluded there was no one about. So far, so good. I made my way through that room and then was presented with a large square door. It automatically opened as I approached it and within a couple of strides, I was stood in an empty corridor. It seemed quiet, now all I needed to do was find the labs and rescue the FPO.

The scans we had taken of the ship from orbit had not been terribly revealing about its internal structure however, rather like some of The Union buildings I had worked in, there was a convenient directory just next to the lifts which connected the five floors to each another.

This kindly informed me that I was on level five at the bottom of the ship which was the storage area and the medical lab was on floor four, directly above. The labs were logically located next door to the medical facilities within that region of the ship. Before I had lost consciousness and we had gone on-board, we all agreed that the hangar at the stern of the ship where the scout ships were parked would be a sensible place to meet to make our escape. I summoned the lift and a few moments later I was on my way toward the medical bay — there were a few people about but no one paid any attention to me as it appeared that I was heading there for ongoing treatment. I walked into the main doctors' area and past the empty reception into the chemistry part. There was no sound anywhere, it seemed that my friends from Ventos had managed to distract the personnel so I could get in. Next to the chemistry department were the biology labs and it did not take me long to find the relevant section. The door was open and a couple of unconscious guards were tied up in the corner. The musclebound man from Ventos had clearly been at work. The perimeter of the lab was benched in the standard layout with white pristine looking worktops. These were littered with useful looking bits of laboratory equipment which I ignored. In the centre of the room, given pride of place was a large bioplastic tank. There were a battery of UV lights switched on above it and, to be honest, it looked far better than it had done the last time I had seen it. As I approached, it turned round and squeaked at me excitedly. I lifted the bioplastic lid off, put my arm inside and let it walk onto my hand. It buzzed happily and snuggled into the palm of my hand. As I stroked the back of its body, it relaxed. Once it settled, I quickly and carefully popped it into my pocket where it stayed still and quiet. I then turned around and headed out of the lab walking quickly and quietly along the main corridor.

Chapter seven – Reckoning and preparations

I walked as nonchalantly as possible along the corridor and back towards the lift I had used earlier. Just as I pressed the button to summon it, there was the tell-tale lurch indicating that the ship had begun to make its descent into the atmosphere. Although the path to the landing bay had been cleared by my friends from the dome on Ventos, at least I would not now need to steal a scout ship. I got into the lift and it descended quickly to level five. I returned the way I had come and ran along the corridor back to the makeshift morgue and climbed carefully back into the coffin. The FPO clambered out of my pocket and sat on my chest wiggling its prongs about and making puzzled sounding noises. I shushed it a couple of times but it ignored me and continued being vocal for some time. However, any sounds must have been drowned out by the sound of the main landing thrusters as the ship descended through the atmosphere. The poor animal seemed to calm down once it had been in the coffin for a few moments and it gave no more puzzled squeaks. We lay, in silence, waiting for the ship to land. After a few moments, the ship gently settled on the ground with a light bump. Obviously, I couldn't be sure exactly where we were but it was obvious they must have found a large flat area of land on which to land.

I lay still in the coffin barely breathing and listened out for sounds from elsewhere. After what seemed like an eternity, the lid was lifted open and Elouisa stood beaming at me by the light of a small torch.

"Let me help you out of there," she said, her smile widening as she saw the FPO.

"Aww, what a sweet little thing! Did you give it a name?"

"No," I said, "I couldn't think of one, I've always referred to it as the FPO. Never thought I'd call it anything."

"From what you've said, it's clearly intelligent." She paused fractionally, "And it likes you," she said in a slightly embarrassed manner, "so it must be alright."

She then passed me my coat which I put on with an immense feeling of relief. At least I would no longer be cold and it gave good cover to a blush that crept over my damaged face. Luckily, the burns mask further obscured this from her. In the awkward silence that followed, I levered myself out of the coffin while Elouisa held the little green creature gingerly in her hands.

"Perhaps I should've called it something...but I'm not sure what." I said nervously and then tried to scratch my chin in what I thought would be a thoughtful and enigmatic way but the effect was somewhat spoiled again by the scraping sound of my finger nails on the burns mask.

"Let's get out of here," she said, changing the subject quickly.

"Righto," I replied, feeling rather relieved.

The Ventos Conspiracy 2

She passed the FPO back to me and I stowed it safely in my coat pocket.

We left the makeshift morgue and headed left along the main corridor. While we headed sneakily along, she explained that six of our little band, after being discharged from the medical unit and being passed as fit for duty, had left the ship and were headed back towards the old dome in a scout ship to see if there was anything salvageable from the base. They were accompanied by a number of security staff, just to ensure they behaved themselves. The remaining members had remained on board to create suitable distractions so that I could rescue the FPO. As we neared the back end of the ship and the hangar, a loud siren started up so clearly, that final part of the plan had only worked for a short time.

We increased our pace and ran along the last stretch of the corridor. At the end was a large door with a tangle of messy wires where the opening mechanism should be – it looked like one of the engineers had done their part of the job properly. We ran through into the hangar. There were six identical ships, all similar in construction to *The Cowrie*. We approached the nearest one just as a group of Union guardians entered the hangar and began to run towards us yelling at us to stop. I grabbed Elouisa's hand and we sprinted together across the hangar to the nearest one. The escape hatch at the stern was open so we ran up the ramp and leapt in. I ran to the front cockpit while she closed off the hatch and then she joined me in the front, at the weapons console.

"Can you fly one of these things?" she asked breathlessly.

"Yes", I said gasping for breath as I buckled myself in, "it's almost identical in configuration to *The Cowrie*." I started up the manoeuvring thrusters.

"Can you use the weapons system?" I asked.

"Yes, it's almost identical to one of my 3D computer games on Earth!" she replied sarcastically.

We lifted off and I swung the stern of the ship around just as the Guardians opened fire, she returned fire using the main rear cannons on the ship. She was an excellent shot and carefully aimed just shy of their position and, with a few carefully placed blasts, managed to drive them back as far of the door which I then destroyed with one of the lasers. They wouldn't be able to get in for a minute or two which would give me time to fly us out of the bay doors at the back of the ship. Which were closed.

"Shit!" I exclaimed. "The bay doors are closed!"

"Don't worry," she said sweetly "looks like this ship is also equipped with missiles." She looked round at me, smiled cheerily and then announced heroically:

"This could be a bit messy" and buckled herself in.

The first missile blasted out of the left hand side of the launcher, shortly followed by a second from the right. The missiles exploded simultaneously in a huge orange ball of flame, just as the Guardians broke through the melted door and opened fire on the ship. At the same time, I fired the main thrusters and the ship shot across the hangar towards the now mostly destroyed doors. In seconds we were out in the clear air and flying away from the ship. I flew our ship around in a large arc and Elouisa opened fire on The Union ship, firstly targeting the engines with the remaining missiles so it wouldn't be able to follow us. It occurred to me that over the last few months, I'd found myself in a number of situations where I'd been forced to open fire on my enemies but I had never thought I would ever see someone else do that with such relish. She positively grinned as pieces of metal were forcibly separated from the ship and little fires and explosions went off all over the place. Although the damage was probably superficial, she seemed to be enjoying herself immensely. The whoops and laughs were quite unexpected too, as were the comments like "Take that you bastards!", "Up yours, you bunch of Johnsons!" and "Leave me to die on a fucking ball of ice, will you?" and so on. It was all faintly amusing at first but, not long afterwards another four of the ships exited the rear end of the ship and began to bear down on our position, clearly ready to attack. Three of them remained on our tail while the fourth flew off in the opposite direction. This didn't strike me as odd, just unexpected.

"What's going on?" asked Elouisa as the three remaining ships launched a full out assault on our ship.

"Not a clue!" I yelled as I swooped low towards the ice so that it sprayed up into the way of the ships behind us before banking, hard right and arcing round behind one of them and shooting the wing off. I then swung round to the left and into a steep climb which allowed the ships to continue to follow. I levelled out in the lower atmosphere and then dived down again, heading straight towards the ground. At the last second, I flipped the engines into reverse and turned the ship around, while Elouisa fired everything we had at our opponents who were now in front of us.

"Chickens! Bastards! Yonks!" she yelled as two of them peeled off and flew around for another pass. The third tried to peel off, out of the dive but collided with a mountain and exploded.

"One down." she said. "Nice flying!"

"Nice shooting!" I replied grinning under my mask.

The other two ships held back slightly, obviously trying to see what we were doing but I set the engines to maximum and headed back over towards the main ship while Elouisa set about continuing her mission of systematically crippling it. As we flew over for another pass, we could see people streaming out from the emergency escape hatches.

The remaining two ships resumed their attack on us, spinning off in all directions whilst firing. Our ship took some considerable damage and it was beginning to look a little like the cockpit of the crashed *Cowrie* did on the Isle of Wight due to all the red lights. Suddenly, there was the welcome sight of *The Cowrie* herself as she flew over the crest of the mountains and engaged the other ships. There was a crackle from the communications systems and a familiar voice came over the intercom.

"Hi Paul and Elouisa, its Jodie and Carlos. Sorry we took so long, we had to take out the other ship first!"
Jodie then swung the ship around in a wide curve and destroyed the ship on our starboard side with a brief burst of laser fire.
"Impressive." I said.
"Ta. I really like the improved weaponry on your ship!" she said as she pulled the ship around to face the final remaining antagonist.
"Thanks, it took me a while to figure it all out." I said modestly.

We sped away, with the enemy ship on our tail and Jodie in pursuit of them. We headed for a deep canyon between two large peaks. As I got to the end of the canyon, I spun the ship round so that our antagonist was trapped between us, pinned down. Jodie then brought *The Cowrie* round in a tight turn, launched a missile at one of the peaks and brought down an avalanche upon it. As we flew off in opposite directions, it was lost in the swirls of snow and did not re-emerge. Once clear of the mountains, we rendezvoused and flew back to the big ship. We could see the smoke for kilometres, and, as we got close, we noted that all around there were survivors. From the condition of the ship, it was clear that it would never fly again. We then turned tail and flew back to the dome. The first thing I did when we landed was remove my friendly FPO from my pocket where it had lain quietly, wisely keeping its head down. I found the old tank it had lived in and put it safely in there. I would have to decide what else to do later on.

Over the next few hours, we returned several times and dropped supplies and emergency kit for the survivors, they were not really responsible for the intended carnage on the planet, that lay directly at the feet of the professor and the higher level cohorts within the Union.

We finally landed outside the cracked dome that my friends had called home since they were abandoned. We stood still for a few moments in silence while I waited for someone to say something. Jodie spoke first, not in a heroic manner but more of a resigned, relieved way that conveyed a little of the gravity of the situation. We may have a brief respite before The Union forces would return, probably in far greater numbers, to try and wipe us, and the FPOs out. We had maybe three or four weeks to get ready. Between us, we took an inventory: twelve humans, five hundred and thirty three FPOs, one semi stable habitation dome, one iced over and windy planet, several dozens of survivors who would probably be out to kill us and two ships, both of which needed extensive repairs.

In the meeting after our confrontation, it occurred to me that there may well be potentially thousands or even millions of the FPOs on the planet. However, we could not save them all and the best we could do was to rescue those that we already had and hope we could use these as a diversion so The Union would leave the remainder of them alone. Scanners were clearly not able to determine the difference between the green and red varieties and so, if we chose to try and save more, we stood a very real chance of running into the vicious variety rather than the friendly one. My new found friends agreed with this and so we decided to stay put and repair things here before figuring out how to deal with the potentially huge numbers of FPOs that remained outside in the cold. As for my pet, I decided the best course of action was to let it join the remaining hibernating FPOs in the freezer. As I hunkered down in front of the freezer and gently pushed it towards the doors, it somehow seemed to understand what I wanted it to do. It slowly shuffled towards the chilly interior and, just as it got to the threshold, it paused and turned around to look at me. I waved at it and said mournfully that I would see it again soon. I found it hard to stop myself from shedding a tear at the departure of my stalwart companion. Once it had gone inside, I shut the doors gently. I sat and watched the temperature indicator as it slowly climbed down to minus five degrees Celsius and then I turned away sadly. At least it was safe for now and with its brethren.

It seemed wise to allocate the tasks to those who were the most experienced so the engineers set to work repairing the ships. Luckily, within the dome were plenty of materials which could be repurposed and used to facilitate repairs. Regarding the ships, due to the duplicate systems, within a few hours and with everyone helping, these were fully operational again. They even refuelled the emergency crash foam on *The Cowrie* as part of the work which was a great personal relief to me as something told me I might well be needing it again. After that, the remainder of the team set about making the dome secure and defendable. Jodie, to her delight, was in charge of weaponry and quickly interfaced several new laser cannons to the power grid, causing it to fail almost immediately. Clearly the power drain from these was too great. If we didn't get the power back on quickly, we could all potentially freeze to death within a few hours. To investigate the damage to the dome, Carlos flew *The Cowrie* within the dome to see if the enormous crack could be repaired from the inside.

However, it became clear from his observations that this would not be possible.

We met in the recreation area and sat around a large square table. While the others urgently discussed how to solve the power problem, a plan began to form in my mind. We needed some form of shielding and there was plenty of that, hidden in the tunnels near where I had lived. We decided that Elouisa and I should go and get that whilst the others repaired the dome.

Elouisa and I took the stolen Union ship and headed back to the settlement to retrieve the remainder of my equipment, the shielding and the remaining supplies from the house and the tunnel system. We talked incessantly on the flight over which took a few hours. It turned out that she was originally from just outside Manchester and had been trained by The Union as a chemist following her compulsory schooling. She too had done a stint of mining on Ceres but a couple of years after I had left. She had also volunteered for the mission to Ventos as she thought the whole idea would be terribly exciting. I mentally noted that this would explain was why she wasn't wearing a bracelet. As she talked, she explained that she had been so engrossed in her work that she hadn't realised the end game for the metallic ore she had been working with. This had changed after she saw several of the more recalcitrant workers being forced to wear bangles or necklaces and noted their subsequent changes in behaviour. She was clearly stuck and so had reluctantly continued her work, even though she realised it was detrimental to the health of some of the workers. She had perpetrated a couple of minor sabotages of her own as an act of defiance.

About half way to the site of the town, she asked me how I had not gone mad in my time alone on the planet and when I explained, she was particularly impressed with my TBR pile and joked that she would like to borrow the book on Aardvarks as it sounded interesting. As we talked the conversation moved on to something that had been bothering me for some time.

"How come the dome was able to operate on a normal twenty four hour cycle, just like on Earth?" I asked in between sips of Tealog.

She laughed musically and leaned back in her chair and then explained that The Union had decided as the day on Ventos was twenty two hours, if they shaved a few minutes off each hour, making each hour shorter, then the maths would work out. So the 1440 minutes usually in a day on Earth was reduced by two hours' worth (one hundred and twenty minutes) and that remaining total of 1320 minutes was divided by twenty four meaning that each hour was fifty five minutes long. It seemed logical as it was only five minutes shorter than at home and the effect on the workers had been minimal.

"I also sabotaged the time system several times in order to upset the mining operation," she continued thoughtfully "and they never guessed it was me."

She smiled radiantly at this memory and then continued cheerily that she thought it meant everyone here was better remunerated than their equivalents back on Earth as they were paid by the hour which, was shorter than at home. We both found this rather amusing and had a bit of a laugh about it while my stomach did a few nervous loop-the-loops.

I left her reading my journal for a few moments while I fetched another cup of Tealog. When I returned, she began asking questions and for clarification of things she didn't understand. I also elucidated on the other animals I'd encountered and she was especially interested in the defensive capabilities of the FPOs and the fact that they were able to defend themselves from the giant slime trailing leaving monsters in the lava tubes. Time passed and we continued to chat pleasantly as we drank further cups of Tealog and the autopilot flew us unmolested, over the snow covered planet.

The town was predictably thickly covered over with snow and only the tallest structures were visible peeping out above the surface. Luckily, the EM fields given off by my perimeter defences made it simple to locate the house itself and a few blasts of the mining lasers cut a wide, deep channel in the snow at the front of the house so that we could get in unimpeded.

As expected, the front door of the house was smashed in. The Union had broken in and trashed the house. Debris was strewn around and the whole place had been turned over for anything useful. They had clearly had fun shooting at things as well as the inside walls were melted and pock-marked with laser fire. They'd also torn up some of the fixtures and fittings that had been present when I had arrived. It was most upsetting to see my former home mistreated in such a manner and seeing it like this made me angry for the first time in quite a while. I stood there and trembled furiously as I surveyed the mess.

"How do we get to the tunnel?" asked Elouisa, clearly sensing that I was angry and trying to take my mind off it.
"I'll show you," I said curtly and, with that, I marched purposefully over to the alcove and descended the couple of floors down to the tunnels. She followed me along with a follower a few seconds later.
"That was fun," she said, "but it made my stomach lurch as we descended and I feel a bit ill now."
"Don't worry," I responded. "You'll get used to it after a few attempts."

The basement was even messier than the rest of the house – they had literally torn everything apart and the defence systems I had carefully integrated were now in pieces and scattered liberally around.

"Bastards," I muttered as I looked at the chaos. Elouisa said nothing but patted me softly on the shoulder in a comforting manner.

The tunnel that I had booby trapped and had led to Scarface's injuries months ago was only slightly blocked with debris and it was a quick job to clear the mess so we could get into the main passageway. I felt better once I was away from the devastation of the house and we jogged along for a couple of kilometres talking incessantly about everything under the suns until we got to the alcoves in which I had hidden much of my stuff. Between us and the follower, we managed to carry just about everything and then we made our way back to the house, on the way stopping off to look at the burial chamber which she found fascinating. She suggested at some point it would be worth making a study of the death rituals of the creatures to which I responded that she was welcome to do that but I would not be joining in. Scarface and his cronies, despite their lack of decency, had not seen fit to desecrate the tombs and had left everything as I had found it, either that or they'd not got that far into the tunnels.

Back in the basement of the house, I quickly showed Elouisa how I had integrated my Earth technology to the geothermal power systems. Although she could not see what I had done as it was ruined, she was most impressed with my engineering skills. "Not bad," was her frequent response. After making sure we had as much useful equipment as we could carry, we left the remains of the house. I suspected that I would not be returning and it was with some considerable sadness that I boarded the ship and we set a course for the dome. By now, it was mid-afternoon and just visible through the snow flurries, the suns were beginning their downward descent over the ice fields. Elouisa flew this time while I tinkered about with the shielding net in an effort to figure out how it could be integrated into Earth power systems. I failed somewhat spectacularly as I was unable to even generate a spark of life from it. Elouisa said she would have a look when we landed as it as it might be a chemistry related problem.

We returned to the dome as quickly as we could and touched down on the beach landing strip just as the light began to drain from the sky. The new provisions from my house were quickly distributed amongst those who could use them best. It occurred to me that the most efficient way to patch up the dome would be to assemble the shielding net over the crack. Luckily, I had been able to grab enough area to more than cover the hole so it was now just a case of figuring out how to connect a power supply to run it. Elouisa and I worked on it together but after hours of head scratching, it was getting rather late and clearly time for a break and some food. Our dinner was a ramshackle affair, especially as the power was still out. Between them however, the engineers Ant (the muscular one) and his friend Zelda were able to rig up a portable power supply from the ships which connected to the ovens so at least we could eat hot food.

After a brief stop, everyone continued to work as fast as they could, despite the rapidly dropping temperatures. Fortunately after much struggling around 23:30, the generators were brought back on line and the temperature slowly began to climb again. Once this was done I explained to the three engineers how the geothermal power system that I had built in the crater worked. Before long, between the four of us, we rigged up a similar system to connect to the main power systems and thus the energy deficit was alleviated. This system was slightly different as it ran off superheated water piped directly from the crust of the planet. The presumed meteor impact had clearly disturbed the crust as the thermal gradient here, beside the huge body of superheated water, was far greater than it had been out on the plains. The steam generated was able to be used to drive the turbines and this system was far more efficient than what I had been able to tap into in my time in the crater. Finally, much later, Jodie and Ant volunteered to keep watch and the rest of us returned to the sleeping quarters. I found a small room off the main corridor in the male section of the habitation block which had a very comfy bed and laid down and quickly fell asleep.

Everyone was woken up at the crack of dawn the following day by the domes internal alarm system which had been set by one of our party to wake up everyone. No-one was happy about this as most of us were still exhausted from the labours of the previous day. However, following a quick breakfast, our work continued rapidly on the geothermal system, tweaking the initial rig and using superconducting filaments that made it far more efficient than the version I had made months before. There was a nerve-racking period while we tested it by passing the generated current through some of the smaller pieces of equipment within the dome. Once we were happy that it was functional and safe, it was connected up to the shielding net. Elouisa had lain awake half the night trying to figure out how this worked and she had several theories which she tried in sequence. Her copious notes on rewritable paper looked like total gibberish to me but she obviously knew what she was doing as on the third attempt (she insisted that she had many other potential solutions), the power began to flow in a safe and controlled manner. Much later, she did try to explain her notes to me but, to be honest, I didn't understand the half of it. Meanwhile, using *The Cowrie*,

The Ventos Conspiracy 2

Carlos and Jodie laser spot welded the shielding net across the crack, stretching it taut across the split from top to bottom and left to right. Once this was complete, they landed on the beach and re-joined us all to witness the switching on of the shields. At first nothing much happened but slowly a reddish light washed upwards from the points where the power conduits had been connected. The thing hummed with a pleasant note which sounded like an A flat. After a minute, to test it, I experimentally threw a rock at it and it bounced off and landed a few metres away. We all cheered and then Jodie and Carlos went off for a well needed rest. Someone else would need to take the next night shift.

With the shielding up and running and the possibility of no more snow or any undesirables getting in, the next job was fill in all of the holes in the outer edge of the dome where the conveyer belts and other services had run. This was relatively easy and the scientists and engineers worked jointly on it, cleverly rigging up some electrified booby traps so that if anyone tried to get in, they would know about it. We collectively dragged some large steel plates across the main entrance and configured them to be opened automatically from the inside. By the end of the second day, the dome was fully intact and the temperature had climbed to a much more respectable twenty one degrees Celsius. Now, with the front door and any entry points sealed, we could properly fortify the space. Elouisa had proven to be pretty handy with weapons too and, leading on from Jodie's work of the previous day, she managed to integrate even more externally mounted lasers to the power supply. These were flown into place by Dave and Matt using the stolen Union ship while we all worked on the power system integration. As a precaution, that afternoon, we stun mined the beach with low voltage devices, just in case they attempted a frontal assault. Pennie was extremely helpful all throughout this process as, being a personal assistant, she was used to organising schedules. She also maintained a list of the jobs which had been done and those which needed doing and, over the coming days, the second list grew gradually shorter and shorter.

After a week of hard work and preparation, we were as ready as we would ever be and coincidentally, it was also time to remove my burns mask. Hannah, who was a doctor by training, had been monitoring the healing process all week and pronounced that this would be safe. So, that morning, I walked into her office in the medical block and she set to work removing the thing. This was a complex process as it was designed to integrate itself into the top layer of my skin so all the individual blood vessel connections had to be disconnected, one by one in the correct order or else I would end up bleeding profusely from many wounds. Each vessel was laser cauterised and sealed over with a super-fast medical grade version of temposkin which would secure the endings of the blood vessels and ensure that no leakages occurred. The whole process took her just over an hour and at the end of it, she showed me my reflection in a mirror. Aside from the slightly off colour patches where the temposkin was attached, I looked the same as I had done before the accident in the ship. She encouraged me to test my facial expressions to see it was ok. So I grinned, stuck out my tongue and rolled my eyes. Nothing hurt and she examined me further and concluded that everything was fine so I left the consultation room feeling better than I had done in weeks. I was also delighted to learn that now that my skin surface had been properly repaired, my hair would grow back. She advised me not to shave for a fortnight at the risk of upsetting the skin but after that, I would be fine. Obviously, my hair would grow back in due course along with my eyebrows. After some final checks, I returned to my friends and we continued to work on little odds and ends that needed doing to complete the repairs and upgrades to the ships, the dome and the defences that we had put in place. When I saw her later on, Elouisa said that I looked much better than I had done earlier which, for some unaccountable reason, made me feel even happier.

It was about 19:00 on the eighth day when the newly installed perimeter scanners picked up a large group of individuals approaching the dome along the beach. As there were no scanner readings from orbit and reinforcements from Earth would not have had time to get here, the only logical conclusion were that they must have been the survivors from the ship we had disabled and secondly, they were all military personnel. The stun mines, along with the motion activated lasers would hopefully prevent anyone from getting too close. However, if they did, we would be in serious trouble as the life signs we detected indicated there were fifty of them, heavily armed and marching in formation. Through the polyscope, in binocular mode, I could tell that at the head of them was a familiar face, it was Tollie from the Mickleover Union dome and he looked murderous.

They were within five hundred metres of the opening of the dome when the first of the stun mines went off. Immediately, half a dozen of the soldiers were immobilised and the remainder fell back and split into two groups. One group attempted to approach from the cliff edge and were stopped by the warning shots from the laser cannons and the other group headed towards the foreshore, hoping to avoid the mines. However, Jodie had suspected that they might try something like this and had mined as close to the water as she dared. Anyone trying to swim round would probably have been boiled alive by the superheated waters of the ocean or eaten by the giant sea monster I had encountered previously. We sat glued to the monitors looking at their futile struggles from the confines of the main control centre and happily noted as every attempt that they made to get to us, failed. Even from our control centre, we had determined that Tollie was clearly in charge as we could hear his dulcet tones echoing around as he yelled at people.

We ate our dinner gathered in the main control centre, intently watching exactly what our protagonists were doing. There was little activity visible as they had obviously given up for now and fallen back and regrouped. The mines had served their purpose. The troops could not get any closer to us so they had set up a makeshift camp in plain sight on the beach. Now, as we scrutinised the monitor, Tollie emerged from a large tent, walked as close to the mines as he safely could and stopped and sat down on the beach. He then drew a portable communication device from his backpack. The corresponding unit within our dome crackled into life:

"Paul Heath, I know that you're in there, come and talk to me. Now." he added aggressively.

I picked up the receiver and replied cheerfully.

"Oh, ciao you old fiore. How's it goin'?"

"Listen to me you arrogant little fucker," he sneered bringing his ugly face and bald head closer to the screen.

"I'm going to kill you in the most painful way I can think of and I'm gonna really, really enjoy it."

"Well, you goat molesting, turd eating, five star fuck up, you tried to destroy me once before and that failed and now you say you'd like to try and have another go? You'll have to catch me first!" I replied brightly.

He harrumphed an unintelligible reply so I continued in the same cheerful tone:

"Fuck off home before I come over there and kick your arse so hard you'll not know what's hit you!"

"Nope," he said. "You see, it's not just me that wants you dead," he continued, even more furiously than before. "I've got an old friend of yours here too – it's Townsend who is now profoundly deaf in one ear thanks to your little green creature."

"That's her fault," I replied loud enough so that everyone in the vicinity could hear. "She's an evil bitch! I also wonder if your Herbert the brain hamster is also perhaps a little deaf, so I tell you again, fuck off back to your tent before I come over there and kick both of your arses from here to the first planet in this system!"

I turned off the communicator and grinned at the others present and said in a merry tone:

"He doesn't like me very much, does he?"

Elouisa was the first to speak and when she did, she was clearly absolutely furious.

"You're a total prick Paul, why do you insist on poking the bear? He's clearly a complete bloody psycho, we're vastly outnumbered and pinned down in here so if he gets inside, we're all going to end up dead."

"It's fine," I replied calmly. "He can't get in. We've got this place locked down tighter than a drum."

"That's not the damn point!" she responded angrily. "Have you ever read anything about sieges? He just needs to sit out there until we either starve or, more likely until the remainder of the forces arrive," she continued breathlessly, "and once they do, we really are totally screwed. They could attack us from orbit and easily destroy the dome – you've said you've seen what a tornado can do to these domes, they're not that strong!"

I thought for a minute and then said much more quietly.

"Yes, sorry all of you, I lost my temper there. I am sorry, really I am. But the fact remains that he wants me dead and he's not going to stop trying to kill me whether he's being all friendly or raving mad. The end result will be the same. We have enough supplies to last us months and we also have a shield, albeit one which only covers part of the dome, but we also have five hundred and thirty three FPOs! I've seen what those things can do! They are phenomenally mean fighting machines when riled, all we need to do is make them cross and they will take care of the rest."

It was Elouisa's time to respond quietly this time, she peered out the window, thought for a second and then said in a slightly menacing tone:

"I'm sorry Paul but that's not good enough. You're going to entrust all our lives to little green monsters from an alien planet that are currently in the deep freeze."

"Yes, I am." I said simply.

"Fine!" she said and stormed off, rapidly followed by the other members of the team.

Some half an hour later, it was Sven, the Norwegian mortician, who came back to speak to me. He was usually a man of few words but when he did, his English was superb. He also looked very nervous and uncomfortable.
"Paul?" he asked carefully, peering round the door.
"Hmm, what?" I replied, picking moodily at my fingernail.
"You need to go and talk to her. Now. I've had experience of this sort of situation, you need to sort it out. She is, how you say it... bonkers about you and I can see that you feel the same way. Go and sort it out before she ends up hating you before you've even given each other a chance."
I looked up and stood there looking at him for a minute. He radiated complete honesty and his serious face was completely expressionless. To be honest, I'd been feeling rather ill at ease since our argument. I have always hated arguing as it is a waste of time and energy and it seemed like he had a good point. I didn't say anything, I just nodded slowly and walked out of the room.

I headed out into the open space outside the central control centre and looked around. I made my way slowly around the whole perimeter of the dome looking for her but she was nowhere to be found. She wasn't with the other scientists who were working on boosting the efficiency of the water reclamation plant, or with the engineers who were adjusting the attenuation on the shield and trying to find ways of increasing its strength. She wasn't back in the control centre with Dave and she wasn't even in the medical unit talking to Hannah with whom she seemed to be friendly. Eventually, as a few meteors flew overhead in the darkness, I headed to the production facility lab where I had first seen her. I made my way in through the main doors and through into the vast silent space. In the distance, I could see that a light was on in the lab so I walked towards it. She was sat on an uncomfortable looking lab chair dictating furiously into her notebook. She looked up at me as I knocked gently on the door. She looked angry, upset and sad all at the same time.

"Er, hi, Elouisa," I said nervously waving my right hand at her.

She did not reply and stared moodily at her notes as if willing them to swallow her up. I continued slowly and carefully.

"I came to um... apologise for being a complete idiot earlier on. I really am very, very sorry. I've been on my own for so long on this planet that I've forgotten how to be part of a social group and how to speak to people. I should have listened to what you were saying earlier and I really am profoundly sorry for being such an arse."

"S'ok," she said sniffily, still not looking up from her work.

"Um," I asked nervously, the feelings that had been developing inside me since I'd first seen her finally making themselves fully apparent, "I wonder if you might erm...join me for a drink in the bar so we can sort this out properly. Please?" I asked pleadingly.

"Yes Paul, I will," she said seriously. "But on one condition."

"Sure." I said questioningly while the butterflies in my stomach starting jumping about like children who'd eaten too much sugar at a party,

"What's that?" I said, trying to keep the happiness and relief out of my voice.

"Stop behaving like a spoilt child and like this situation only affects you. We're all here, we're all trying to stay alive and we're all trying to help one another."

She finally looked up at me and said defiantly, "Get that into your head and we'll be fine."

I nodded and she stood up from her chair and smoothed down the front of her labcoat before removing it and hanging it back on the peg from which it came. The pair of us then walked out of the lab saying nothing.

We entered the almost empty bar which was manned by Sven. Most of the remainder of the group were on guard duty however, we did find Jodie necking pints with Dave and making a lot of noise about it. We ignored them and walked over to a quiet corner on the opposite side of the bar and sat down in the snug, on different sides to one another. I've never been much of a drinker and, coupled with the fact that I was terribly nervous and hadn't had a drink since Cambridge, my alcohol tolerance was ridiculously low. Hers, on the other hand, was much higher. She had drained her third glass of red wine by the time I'd finished my first pint.

We'd not said much but, armed with the brain numbing effect of alcohol we finally started talking, initially about nothing much in particular. In addition to what I already knew, I learned that she had a sister who was three years older than she was, that her parents had been scientists and that her uncle had been high up in the science department at the Cheshire local laboratories and that she hated cherries in any form. As the evening wore on and the empties built up, we gradually relaxed and things felt a bit more normal. Just after the clock above the bar struck 1am, Jodie threw up all over Dave, who found this hilarious and then he too passed out, hitting his head softly on the table. I stopped talking, squinted slightly drunkenly at my chronometer and managed to say something like "It's getting a teensy-weensy bit late, I think we should be going to bed" and I don't recall much after that.

I awoke sharply with the alarm the following morning with a raging hangover and my face aching quite badly. As I looked around blearily, trying to focus, I realised that I wasn't in my room. The décor gave it away that I was in the female only part of the accommodation block. As I lay there trying to think, the sound of a shower from the adjacent bathing area, accompanied by some rather impressive singing of a recognisable tune from one of Schubert's many lieder, informed me that Elouisa was in there and clearly feeling absolutely fine. She emerged from the bathroom a few seconds later with a large towel wrapped around her middle and grinned at me.

"Oh, you're awake, that's good Paul. How's the head?"

I looked blankly at her.

"That bad?" she laughed musically and went back into the bathroom. I wished she hadn't as her laugh echoed round my mind like a bell. She returned shortly after, sat demurely on the edge of the bed and passed to me, along with a glass of water, two small green coloured tablets.

"Take those and you'll be right as rain in a few minutes. We've got work to do."

I nodded which was a terrible idea as I thought my face would fall off and so I quickly swallowed the tablets and collapsed back into the bed and lay there until the drugs kicked in. She wasn't wrong as within about ten minutes, I felt pretty much like myself.

Elouisa and I returned to my quarters so that I could change and take some anti-inflammatory tablets for my painful face and then we headed to the canteen for breakfast. Now that the work on the dome had been completed and Tollie and his soldiers were safely stuck behind a minefield with no chance of attacking, people who weren't on guard were milling around talking and laughing. As we entered the room hand in hand, six pairs of eyes swivelled round to look at us. We let go of each other and tried to look less embarrassed than we actually were. The remaining two pairs were hard to see as they belonged to Dave and Jodie and were hidden behind dark glasses – clearly the anti-hangover drugs had their limits. I could hear that a few comments were made quietly between various people but tactfully ignored them.

We had just started our breakfast when Maria ran breathlessly into the canteen and announced that something was happening with the soldiers. En masse, we all stood up and headed quickly to the control centre. On the main screen, we could see that behind the fifty or so individuals, a converted ship had hoved into view, crawling very slowly along the beach.

Ant, who had been the other one on guard duty was the first to speak.

"Shit, looks like they must've been able to retrieve that final ship from the main attack vessel and convert it to ground operating mode."

Zelda, who was one of the engineers and one of the quieter members of our party then asked cautiously if it could survive intact driving over the mines.

"Yes, probably." replied Elouisa.

"Bollocks," said Dave. "We're in trouble then, aren't we?"

I stood there for a few seconds scratching my slightly stubbly chin thoughtfully.

"No, it's going to be fine, all we need to do is fire up the ships and blow it to bits!"

No-one disagreed and within a few minutes, we had two craft in the air, me piloting one with Elouisa in the co-pilot's seat and Matt and Zelda in the other. Jodie remained in the dome, saying that she would be better off operating the external defence systems.

We flew quickly up into the cloudy sky, veering sharply in formation and then bearing down on the crawling tank like ship as it progressed slowly through the minefield. The soldiers had aligned themselves behind it so as it moved forward, the mines were discharged. They took a few seconds to recharge once triggered but this recharge time was more than enough for the troops to form up smartly behind the ship. Once we started firing upon them, they pretty soon broke rank and were scattered in all directions. Tollie was briefly visible, attempting to direct the terrified people the best places to try to penetrate our defences. He then disappeared behind the lines and out of sight.

His plans of attack were generally not terribly successful, many troops were immobilised by the mines and, as we came round for a pass at the crawling ship, we insured that it took further damage. Suddenly, our attention was diverted by Tollie who had reappeared and now brandished a large and very powerful laser and was taking pot shots at *The Cowrie*. Those left behind at the dome scanned the area and reported to us on both ships that a small group of half a dozen troops had finally managed to get clear of the carnage and were through the minefield and on an intercept course with the main entrance of the dome. Tollie, despite some fairly messy looking injuries, was still clearly furious and in no mood to let those stop him. Townsend also looked similarly determined as she marched up to the gun position he'd set up to join him. Both were heavily armed with a wide selection of nasty looking guns.

I was told later on what had happened to the remainder of the troops in my absence. Jodie and the others who weren't in the ships had quickly headed to the front of the dome and brought the main weapons on line. Tollie and his remaining soldiers had been only about a hundred metres away when they opened fire and they'd continued to advance, closing fast. Jodie had occupied the defensive chair we'd installed on one side of the entrance and opened fire on the soldiers with the pulse laser. Within seconds she had shot two of them but the others spread out and continued to return fire. Dave, sat on the right hand side platform only got one. Neither of them had yet managed to kill Tollie and he continued to skulk behind his gun turret towards the edge of the mine field, like the coward he was, waiting for an opportunity. The remaining solders concentrated their attack on Jodie's position. They were clearly well trained as they knew exactly where to aim and within thirty seconds of their comrades falling, they had disabled the weapon. Dave's gun was their next target and it too was destroyed within a few seconds. Dave was shot in the arm as he bundled out, clear of the fizzing bolts of death. Jodie too was injured, she received a nasty leg wound as a piece of exploding gun hit her. The others extracted them and fell back behind the entrance, which was left open. Carlos and Maria had taken up hiding places either side of the opening, one in the guard post and the other behind a pile of rubble and pieces of masonry. Both of them managed to incapacitate a soldier each which left only Tollie and Townsend. They both held back, using their large laser to take pot-shots. They were now clearly aware of the trap we'd laid inside the dome. My comrades in the dome were all armed to a greater or lesser degree with a mix of proper military weaponry and assorted mining lasers modified to turn them from tools into weapons. However, it was soon clear that these were not really built for prolonged use and one by one, they failed. Tollie had clearly figured this out and was happily hurling insults at them as they had tried in vain to shoot him and Townsend with increasingly unreliable weaponry.

Tollie, for all his numerous faults was clearly a very good shot. We flew over his gun position strafing the area with laser bolts when there was a deeply unsettling noise from the engines. Several of the dreaded red lights flashed brightly and smoke poured from the rear of the ship. We began to lose altitude.

"I'm gonna have to land!" I yelled as a further series of alarms went off.
Elouisa nodded frantically and ran across the cockpit to help me try to control the increasingly erratic flight path of the ship. Luckily, the landing thrusters were undamaged so once we were within landing distance, these were sufficiently powerful to affect a safe, albeit wobbly, uncontrolled landing on the beach.

The ship shook as a series of laser bolts from Tollie's gun drilled some surprisingly impressive holes in the hull. We grabbed a couple of lasers from near *The Cowrie*'s escape hatch and jumped out through it. Somehow, despite all the noise from the battlefield, we could clearly still hear Tollie's rabid yelling. More by luck than good judgement, we'd landed with the airlock facing away from the beach battleground and so we were protected from the increasingly violent volley of shots from both Tollie and Townsend. We made our way carefully around the bulk of the ship and, safely hidden behind the port engine, returned fire. The firefight lasted a few moments but neither of us was making headway. A sudden impressive sounding noise overhead made me look as our other ship, piloted by Matt and Zelda hoved into view. Both Tollie and Townsend were clearly so furious that they had totally forgotten about that and, as we watched, our friends made a low pass over the gun position and, with some excellent shooting, destroyed it. Both Tollie and Townsend were thrown clear by the force of the explosion and lay on the sand, groaning loudly.

Elouisa and I cautiously emerged from behind *The Cowrie* just as the pair of bastards got shakily to their feet and started to fire at us with their hand held weaponry. A lucky shot from Townsend grazed my arm and I felt the characteristic stab of pain which meant the skin was burned. However, we ran forward a few more metres and took up a defensive position behind a large boulder and returned fire. In the ensuing exchange, from our relatively safe position we managed to drive them back, away from the entrance to the dome and from the remainder of our group. Suddenly, in a lull in the shooting, the pair of them looked at each other, nodded and then turned tail and sprinted the last ten metres or so towards the half wrecked crawling ship. We succeeded in getting a couple of shots at them but failed to hit them. They quickly leapt inside via the main entrance, scrambled to the front of the ship and sat down, peering myopically at us through the ruined front screen as we shot ineffectively at them. I could just make out Townsend taking up position at the weapons console and stabbing viciously at the buttons and mouthing some quite filthy language while Tollie tried to get the engines working. The relative peace was shattered by the buzzing sound of the power relays warming up, and then a loud and impressive whine as the main systems came back on line. The ship was pretty much a wreck however the two idiots clearly thought that they could use the main weapons against us. As we watched in horrified silence, a series of small explosions tracked along the hull, in line with the weapon's power conduits and then, in a massive blaze of orange, red and white, the whole thing detonated in a ground shaking explosion that threw us off balance. Just for a millisecond, a crazy plan crossed my mind about trying to save them. However, as the ferocity of the inferno intensified, I realised that would be foolhardy. We grabbed hold of each other to regain our footholds and stood and watched, totally helpless as the ship erupted in a huge gout of flame which lit up the whole area. Bits of melted and mangled metal rained down left and right. No one could possibly have survived the explosion.

After a couple of minutes, we turned our back on the bonfire and I helped Elouisa to carefully make her way back along the beach and met up with Matt and Zelda. They were uninjured and together, the four of us rendezvoused with the remainder of the team who were still unscathed. Hannah was working on both Dave and Jodie's injuries in the medical unit and so did not join us. I insisted she leave my arm alone but I graciously accepted a strip of temposkin which I slapped over the burn and the hole and I also took a dose of painkillers. A little while later, we stood around in a little semi-circle, just outside the entrance to the dome and listened to the fires and debris slowly cooling in the increasingly cold air. The weather seemed to be clearing for the first time in weeks and there was even a faint hint of sunshine as the two flaming orbs dropped slowly towards the horizon. We had won this battle but not the war. The Union were approximately three weeks away and would no doubt be returning in far greater numbers. However, with the immediate threat vanquished, we headed to the bar for a celebratory drink or two.

Some hours later, I left the others to their merrymaking and stood outside in the night air, listening out for anything untoward. Aside from the faint sighing of the wind and the infrequent sounds of meteors shooting across the sky, all was perfectly quiet. Further along the beach, I could see a phosphorescent patch which indicated that the anemones were out and about doing whatever they did at night. Everything seemed peaceful and quiet and I just stood there, enjoying the atmosphere. After a few minutes, I heard footsteps behind me. I turned round quickly but I needn't have worried, it was Elouisa. She walked up to my side and stopped and held out her hand. We stood there together, holding hands and looking up through the dome at the stars and said nothing for a very long time.